GENESIS
a novella
Copyright © G.P. Rice 2025
Peagerm Press
ISBN 978-1-0369-1307-6
contact us at:
peagermpress@gmail.com

GENESIS

It all starts somewhere . . .

1

In the beginning there was a fog, a fog that triggered time and space, from whence I came and shall return to, no doubt none the bloody wiser.

First thing I remember was fear. I was being lowered into something. Something very shiny and cold. My stomach churned as I lay there helpless.

Next, snapshots from a home, it always seemed so drab and grey, a lack of warmth, a lack of space, a lack of something yet to experience. There was a little yard out back, clean but cold, solid brickwork, unforgiving concrete floor, a washing line way up in the sky and a wooden gate that was always bolted. To the right a narrow coal house, next to that the outside toilet, such a harrowing experience, why did anyone have to excrete? The seat was always freezing cold and way too high for kids like me. Mounting it was one thing but retaining a balance was quite another. Plus there'd always be a spider, staring at you, full of menace, often way up in a corner, still, you couldn't help but look. I found it better in the dark, the added fear would get things moving. I'd be in and out in an instant, barely time to pull the chain.

Beyond the gate, a blackened mountain, it stood very tall and wide, shadowing the whole of Grangeworth, waste material from the pit. That was where my father worked, my mother mostly stayed at home, the only times we ventured out were when she'd drag me up to the shops or catch a bus to visit relatives.

Eric Peagerm, that was me, I had an older sister, Judy; soft blonde hair wrapped up in a bow; big brown eyes projecting something I was way too young to grasp. You'd often find us out in the yard, I had a push-cart full of blocks, she had a little pram for her dolls, I seem to remember a tricycle but don't recall who it belonged to. All that space was liberating, it was far too cramped in the house, and scary too from what I remember, thunder, mice, the occasional argument, we were forever hiding from something, huddled up behind the couch.

We had a very small TV, an ancient black and white contraption, didn't watch it very much, I found the programmes quite confusing. Watch With Mother, silly title, she was always way too busy; washing, drying, cooking, cleaning; I'd be sat in perfect silence, gawping at the glowing screen, wondering where our Judy was, no doubt tucked away in school. I could have done with her support, that Andy Pandy, he was creepy, yes, he had a cutesy face, but what was all that stuff he was wearing, he was like a miniature clown, his bland expression never changed, I found him rather sinister. The Flowerpot Men, absolute gibberish, not forgetting Pogles Wood; a cackling witch is what I remember; what the hell were they trying to do to us, keep us riveted in our seats or help us with our bowel movements?

One day there was quite a commotion. "YOU STAY THERE!" my mother screamed. I quickly ran upstairs to the bedroom, something bad had happened, it seemed.

There was a busy road out front, a car had managed to hit our Judy. Broke her leg I found out later. Looking back she'd got off lightly.

2

After that we moved to Trimley, it was like a different world, a quiet little cul-de-sac with fenced-off gardens at the back and unobstructed lawns out front. I liked it, all that greenery, the lawns, the hedges, even trees, beyond them lots of open ground, it all seemed rather nice and tranquil. Inside it was spacious too, you could run around in there, I had a bedroom all to myself, a bathroom just along the landing and next to that an indoor toilet!

    I remember my first day at school, visible from my bedroom window, possibly why I wasn't scared, though schools were often on TV and the kids were always well behaved and fully immersed in rewarding activity. Mother led me by the hand and left me at the teacher's mercy, which was fine, she was nice, I wondered why some kids were crying. This is when I realised that everybody was quite different, grown-ups were unfathomable but surely kids were all the same? Apparently not. Some were screaming, begging parents not to leave, a few were dashing back and forth as I sat waiting for instructions. Next to me was Andy Marshall, he was also my next door neighbour, that seemed fairly reassuring, at least until *his* bowel movements suddenly became an issue. He insisted he went home. Request denied, the school had toilets. "NO!" he screamed, which startled me, but stubbornly he stood his ground and shat in his desk at morning break.

Trimley Infants, it was great, we had a water tank, a sand pit, not sure what the tank was for but me and another kid messed with it and got us into a heap of trouble. We were dispatched to see the Headmistress who whacked our hands with a twelve-inch ruler. Hey, I thought. That's not fair! We were only having fun! I guessed that's why we had a playground, it was twice the size of the school and full of entertaining games with hopscotch, skipping, marbles, tiggy, a cauldron of unbridled energy. Dinner ladies ran the show, they made sure everyone behaved, occasionally they'd shout at you but mostly they were very kind, like older versions of your parents. All the kids were pretty friendly, except for one, Terry Mellows, he had angry-looking eyes and marched around with a sad little posse, intent on exercising authority. He was in the class above, I tried to avoid him as best I could, but he would always stare at you as if you'd somehow done him wrong. Bullies. Wrong'uns. Hated them. Why could they not leave us alone? Some would roam around the streets intent on stirring up some trouble. Older kids would send them packing. "GET BACK ROUND YOUR OWN BLIDDY END!" We'd have to face them back at school but mostly they were kept in check.

I soon discovered my neighbour's pain, the toilet paper was horrendous, it resembled tracing paper, but thicker, it was dangerous! What the hell were they trying to teach us, discipline, thrift, the meaning of pain? None of which I understood, your bottom was a delicate thing, at five years old the world was a puzzle.

Andy and his pooping problems, one day we were out the front, I can't remember what we were doing but suddenly he ran to the door and banged upon it furiously.

It was answered by his dad.

"Whaddya want?"

"A number two!"

"You'll have to wait."

"I can't, I can't!"

"Your mother's busy in the bathroom!"

"But it's coming!"

There was a sigh, he went and got a big white bucket, next I knew I was watching Andy poop a load of faecal matter. It was such an odd experience, gross but rather mesmerising. There was Andy, held aloft, his little arse suspended there as dark brown chods of chocolate fudge emerged from him relentlessly.

I spent a lot of time next door, Andy had a stack of books, his dad was covered in tattoos, but mam seemed nice, a little strange, but otherwise a tender soul. I ran in looking for him one day, his dad was on top of his mam on the couch.

"Hey, what the hell ya doin'?"

"Where's Andy?"

"Well, he's not under here!"

3

I was such a quiet kid, partly nature, partly environment; soon I came to realise that this was not the thing to be. Gobby kids seemed happier, they had more friends, were more relaxed, the others gravitated towards them while I could only stand and watch. My father was the silent type, he always seemed preoccupied, not distant necessarily, but when he did decide to speak you always got the feeling he had something meaningful to say. Some folks never seemed to stop, they rambled on incessantly, my dad however chose his words and everybody seemed to listen. I did *not* know how to speak, I found it hard to express myself, my thoughts were coming thick and fast but when it came to verbalising I was clearly lacking something. Some disturbing things would happen; often, late at night in bed. I'd lie there staring up at stuff, the light shade or the vent perhaps, then all of a sudden, a split second later, I would get a tingling feeling, somewhere near the top of my spine and before I could make any sense of it, I'd find myself up against the ceiling, panic-stricken, feeling trapped. It was scary for a kid, it felt as though I'd left my body, not that I would dare look down, the one time that I did turn round the only thing that caught my attention was all that dust on top of the wardrobe. When the feeling did subside I'd quickly scramble out of bed and either whine at the top of the stairs, or if it was much later at night, I'd leap into my parents bed and scare the living shit out of them. The landing light stayed on after that and the bedroom door would have to stay open. That would help to some degree but sometimes things got *very* weird.

I had this worn old teddy bear, a big one, almost half my size but very pleasing to the touch, especially his velvet paw pads. He would often sleep with me, he had these very knowing eyes, which always seemed to comfort me, it helped to know that he was there.

But one night he did something strange, he whispered softly into my ear. "Eric," he said, "come with me, there's something that I have to show you!"

Oh, I thought, OK Ted, I let him take me by the hand, across the landing, down the stairs, along the passageway into the kitchen.

There we stood at the locked back door. "You'll have to open it," he said. "I'm way too small!"

So was I.

I stood there stretching up on tiptoes.

"Eric! What the hell are you doing?"

"Trying to open the door for Teddy."

Mam just stood and stared at me, then led us both back up to bed.

4

Boynston View was full of kids. Kenny Bevans, next door upwards, he seemed pretty strange at first though not a patch on his nervy sister, his manic mother and weird-looking father. Though his dad was born cross-eyed and marched around like a menacing robot, Kenny was more like a slobbering dog with a permanent dopey grin on his face and a mat of greasy, long black hair which gave him the look of a raggedy spaniel. Next to them we had the Millwards, Karen and Peter, they were nice, then further upwards, Danny Easton, an excitable fantasist who once claimed, with the utmost sincerity, that he'd once met Captain Kirk on a weekend trip to Boston Spa. Then there was the Devanny family, an oddball bunch though not the daughter; Jane was lovely, softly spoken, gently smiled with big, sad eyes the deepest shade of emerald green. Her brother, James, was in my class; tall and stout with thick-lensed glasses, freckled face, straight black hair, square fringe like a lego man. He was pretty quiet too, he would stare off into space but when at last he did pipe up he'd always tell you something strange or something which was way too personal. *"Eric, I've just had a wee."* There was nothing you could say. He would never tell the teacher, he'd just sit there silently while calmly looking straight ahead or fiddling with his chubby fingers, mumbling nonsense to himself. Sometimes he would stop mid-sentence, you'd be hanging by a thread, glad he'd stopped in one sense but then terrified he might continue. He was also prone to fits. That was quite disturbing at first, but what surprised me most was the ambivalent attitude of his mother. Sometimes she would try to soothe him, other times she'd sound annoyed. "Stop it, James!" she'd snap at him, as if he had a choice in the matter. There was no sign of a dad, there was however an angry gran, a toothless, squawking, mad old witch, the type you'd think would live alone with umpteen cats and a misty cauldron.

I was used to erratic behaviour, one of my grandmas lived in Winstone, a psychiatric hospital, apparently the largest in Europe. I remember my first trip there, my mother took me on the bus, the open grounds seemed nice enough but once we'd made it through the treeline we were met by wandering patients. Not just ordinary folk but people plagued with mental problems, you could see it in their eyes, something wasn't right up there. One was gurning like a fool, it seemed as though he couldn't stop, another was grabbing things from the sky, obviously imaginary. Others gave you the strangest stare then strode on by like nothing had happened. Nothing ever did of course but I found the whole thing quite unsettling. It was fear of a different kind, monsters caught you, possibly ate you, but in a strange, demented mind who knew what tortures lay ahead? Imagination was one thing but what of the things you couldn't imagine? It was the fear of the unknown. Winstone Hospital reeked of it. Inside, it was so much worse, the moaning of some stricken soul. Sudden bursts of shouting or screaming, echoing through the corridors. It helped when someone else was there, someone stable to hang on to, Mam was often too upset, you only had to look at her. A lot of times we'd be turned away, whichever family members were there, a doctor or nurse would enter the room with a clipboard or a stack of papers, hardly daring to look at us, an all too familiar look on their face. Gran would be having a 'difficult' day, yet sometimes she would come and greet us, sitting, having cuddled Mam, at a nice little table by the window. She would have a wistful smile, it haunted me, whatever it was. I would ask a lot of questions but would never get an answer. All I knew for certain was she'd been in there for many years, why remained a mystery, I guessed the reasons were too painful. Gran seemed normal enough to me but we only saw her on her good days, what her bad ones may have revealed seemed out of reach to all of us.

5

My mother's father lived in Kelton, that's where she was born and raised, another village, not too far, we visited quite regularly. Granda Busher lived alone, in a terrace up on a hill; Auntie Maisie lived there too, my mother's only other sibling. Auntie Maisie, she was great, a little brash but funny with it, practical and down to earth, completely different to my mother. Mam put on appearances, a lovely smile for those outside but not so much around the house unless we had any strangers in. Her accent was forever changing, why, I didn't understand, I knew what airs and graces were, but still, as far as I could tell, the people who she met outside all spoke with the same old pit village accent. It was slightly different with Dad, his accent did seem naturally softer, not sure why he spoke that way but it was curious nonetheless. Perhaps it was to do with his job, he was now some kind of surveyor, the pit had closed, as most of them had, he'd moved along to pastures new.

We drove to Kelton in the car, along a little country lane, the highlight being a crest in the road which always made our stomachs jump. "Here it comes!" our Judy would say, we'd brace ourselves as we approached, then burst out with a unified "WHOOOOAH!!!" as we sailed on up and over.

Auntie Maisie's house was different, not as neat and tidy as ours, it had a very different smell, not good or bad but noticeable. Their household seemed to mirror ours but everyone was slightly younger, probably coincidence but still it did seem quite uncanny. Dad would sit with Uncle Ryan, always at the kitchen table, Mam and Maisie, they'd decant and have a catch up in the lounge. Judy would escape with Sandie, she was funny, wicked laugh, while I'd be left with little Mikey, it was unavoidable. Small and stout with piercing eyes, bluer than the summer sky, scruffy mop of flaxen hair, the archetypal little scamp. His flattened nose was always running, not that it would bother him, he'd lick the mucus from his lip as if it were a delicacy. Though younger he would take the lead, he was very rough and tumble, he would drag me off somewhere before I had a chance to speak. He'd show me all his latest pets then crash on through the garden gate before scrambling up the side of the pit heap or scooting off down some old track which always seemed to lead to the beck.

Uncle Ryan, he was formidable, very different to my dad, a burly fellow, big round face, occasionally a cheeky smile. He was in the building trade, what exactly I'm not sure, but he and Dad would chat about it, mostly not too favourably. "Alright, young'un?" he would say. I'd just smile quite sheepishly. I got the feeling he thought I was soft. Compared to him, I guess I was. He had lurchers out in the yard, noisy and excitable, and an old Jack Russell, hunting dogs, not the family pets I was used to. Some of his tales were slightly disturbing, like the way he dealt with tapeworms, starving the infected dog before jimmying its jaws open, dangling raw meat over its mouth, until at last, after God knows how long, something stirred in the back of its throat as the ravenous worm began to emerge. It sounded strange but I believed him, what did *I* know about such things, he said he'd wind the head of the worm around a little hazel twig, then drag it from the poor dog's throat like a manky piece of tagliatelle.

Once we had our dinner there and we were served up rabbit pie. Everybody savoured it though little Mikey wasn't happy.

"Better not be one o' mine!"

Once, apparently, it *had* been.

Uncle Ryan glared at him.

"That's what happens when you're bad!"

I got a little taste myself. Mikey wasn't feeling well.

"I know exactly what he needs . . . *taffy!*"

That was black treacle.

Uncle Ryan spooned it down. Little Mikey pulled a face. Then he turned to look at me.

"*YOU* could do with some o' this!"

Next I knew he'd held me down and forced a spoonful into my throat. First it tasted almost sweet but seconds later it turned sickly. Vomiting had crossed my mind but then I thought it best to swallow. Dad just sat and watched it all. I found it so disheartening.

6

Medicines were curious, I do remember quite a few, like Calpol, that was really nice, though Benylin, I'm not so sure. Syrup of Figs was lovely, but I couldn't stomach Cod Liver Oil. Rose Hip Syrup, heaven sent. Milk of Magnesia, from below.

As a child I was often sick. Everybody knew the doctor, kindly fellow, bushy eyebrows, his surgery was down in Grangeworth. You'd be forced to join a queue. Not a line of any sort, just a crowded roomful of illness.

"Who's in last?"

"You're after me."

Other remedies were available, many things to soothe your throat. Fisherman's Friends, Victory V's. Suck on those, you could overcome anything. Taste was quite a potent sense, like all young kids my tooth was sweet. Sherbert Lemons, Dolly Mixtures, couldn't get enough of those. Naturally I loved ice cream but who'd have thought there was so much variety; shops had many different flavours but even the stuff from the ice cream man would come in many different forms. Rossi's, firm, like solid ice, sold by a scrawny guy in his seventies, hollow cheeks but pleasant enough, and who, despite the beret, was Italian. Mr Whippy, soft and creamy, you could have a flake in there, or rainbow sprinkles, monkey's blood, a wafered sandwich or simply a tub. One of my enduring memories is sprinting after the ice cream van, thruppeny bit, held aloft like a magical, mystical golden ticket. Unfortunately I stumbled slightly and lost my grip on that precious coin, which leapt from my despairing fingers, disappearing down the drain.

The worst thing that I ever tasted was out of a bottle at Nanna Peagerm's. She lived just behind the rec with Granda P. and Uncle Robbie. Granda P. was another big chap, a muscular, retired miner, always busy doing things, though sometimes, when his guard was down, he'd stick me on the end of his knee and sing me some of the strangest songs. "When I was a laddie I lived wi' me Ganny" or "I like coffee, I like tea". There weren't *that* many songs in his repertoire but the lyrics were so confusing. "Diddle diddle dumpling, mice and John". What did *mice* have to do with anything? Still, I went along with it all, it did seem like a show of affection.

Anyway, back to the story of Nanna, she had bottles of pop in the kitchen, usually in the cool of the pantry, we would have to ask for it. We'd gulp it down then burp it out. "Gissy pig!" Nanna would say. She gave us liquids full of gas. What were we supposed to do? Still, sometimes the answer was no. "Plenty of water in the tap!" We'd have to sneak behind her back, something she must have cottoned on to. One day it was pretty warm and I'd been running around outside, a glass of pop was just what I needed but since there was no-one around in the kitchen, quite unusual for Nanna's, I thought I may as well skip permission and made a beeline for the pantry. There it was on the concrete floor. Dandelion and Burdock, the best!

Black and sweet and full of flavour, didn't think about a glass. I took a swig and gulped it down and threw it all back up in an instant, coughing and choking, throat burning, I'd just chugged down a mouthful of vinegar!

Nanna's house was a Sunday staple, sometimes Saturday nights as well, our parents often went to the club and left us there with a bag of pyjamas. Me and Judy shared a bed, a big one, it was soft and cosy, then next day, late in the morning, Mam and Dad would make an appearance, followed by a bunch of relatives. Often it was Uncle Tom with Auntie Dora, Kenny and Sam. They lived further north in Shodden, Uncle Tom was Dad's little brother. There was another, Uncle John, but he lived miles away in the Midlands, he'd materialise much less often with Auntie Jean and another three boys, Joseph, Jack and little Matthew. Dad had a younger sister too, Auntie May, who we saw on occasion; she lived on the South-East coast and had a very different accent. Uncle Seth, her stern-looking husband, had a thing against the 'darkies'. Suki and Jade, his two young daughters, teased him about it constantly.

"Seen any *darkies* lately, Daddy?"

"Darkies are *lovely*, don't you think?"

Uncle Seth would look annoyed as the girls just sat there giggling.

Yet teasing in general, didn't like it, not so bad when the girls would do it; Judy and Sandie, Suki and Jade, it seemed to come from a place of fun, but Kenny and Sam and John's three boys, their playful quips were quite relentless, two of them were older than me and always pressing home their dominance.

Which destroyed me, I was fragile, I was barely able to cope, I soon went back inside my shell and the next I knew I was known as the shy one, which would only make things worse. My confidence took quite a hit, our Judy tried to show support but that just made my Nanna angry.

"Toughen up! Shy bairns get nowt!"

It was good without any relatives, Nanna could bake, I'll give her that, the smell of that house on a given Sunday was more than enough to make anyone drool. I'd wander around the kitchen, looking, I'd escape with a butterfly cake. "Hungry Horace!" she'd snap at me, I was either that or Moaning Minnie.

Then we'd wait around for tea, Uncle Robbie smoking his pipe, Mam providing help in the kitchen, Dad immersed in the Sunday papers. I'd be laid there on the carpet, soaking up those black and white movies, Westerns, Comedies, Laurel and Hardy, loved them all, such good, clean fun.

7

In those days we had proper seasons, snow in winter, sun in summer; spring and autumn lots of rain when things were either growing and thriving or dying off in a last splash of colour. When it rained we'd stay at home, we'd read our books or watch TV; sat there, boredom slowly creeping, leaping up to the window when a mobile vendor came around. The ice cream man was most appealing, but there was the fish man, the pop man, the fruit and veg man, the rag and bone man, carting off your unwanted crap in exchange for a handful of pegs or balloons.

    I didn't have a lot of books but those I had I really enjoyed. Aesop's Fables, Grimm's Fairy Tales, some of which seemed pretty dark but they were full of ancient wisdom and always sparked my imagination. Brer Rabbit with its strange illustrations, Nutwood Tales with Rupert Bear. Billy the Badger, Podgy the Pig. Why were there so many talking animals? It was the same thing on TV, cartoons full of wacky characters, Tom and Jerry, Felix the Cat; funny, yes, but often confusing. Some wore clothes while others didn't. Some wore tops but never bottoms. Why? They were just cartoons but little details bothered me. The Flintstones Christmas show for example; wasn't the Stone Age way before Jesus? Pluto, he was Goofy's dog, but wait a minute, what was Goofy? Not to mention

Wile E. Coyote, how did he survive all that? Yes, I know, all part of the joke, but part of my little brain wasn't having it.

Regular shows were a very mixed bag, some of them were beyond confusion, The Singing Ringing Tree for example, what the hell was *that* about? Dubbed (badly) with menacing dwarves; gruff old men in piss-poor bear suits; freaky, metallic, wide-eyed fish. They were insane in Eastern Europe! British shows could be taxing too, especially in black and white, it helped create an atmosphere where warmth and safety weren't an option. Doctor Who, that was strange, part riveting, part terrifying, sure, the monsters could be crap but in tandem with the sound effects the whole thing did feel pretty jarring. Mannequins that came to life and suddenly burst through high street windows, terrorising all and sundry, shooting at people without reason. Shops were suddenly scary places, especially department stores, I looked at people differently and the more I looked the more I feared them. Thank the Lord for Gerry Anderson, long gone were the days of Torchy, now he'd really hit his stride and was churning out some fabulous stuff. Puppets, yes, but that didn't matter, I enjoyed the wit and humour, sometimes quite ridiculous but I loved the campiness of it all. Stingray and the Aquaphibians, Captain Scarlet in all his glory, indestructible, yes indeed, but that was hardly surprising when his main protagonists seemed to be torch lights. Thunderbirds, an excellent show, I had all the die-cast models, 1 through 5, the whole shebang, plus Lady Penelope's pink Rolls Royce! Naturally I worshipped Batman, hilarious yet still exciting, different villains every week, the highlight of a Saturday morning. Star Trek too, I loved all that, imaginative and incredibly hopeful, the enormous potential of space, the Sci-Fi shows enchanted me.

Still, I was an outdoor kid, I'd mostly like to kick a football, must have went through dozens of those, the things were very easy to puncture. Alfie Coombes, a blonde-haired lad, would often come round after tea, we'd both take turns at being in goal while the other practiced shooting skills. The strip of grass out front was ideal, flanked by all the pigeon crees, a wall at the back behind two saplings, acting like a net of sorts behind a couple of natural goalposts.

"Excellent shot!"

"Cracking save!"

We'd always offer words of encouragement, any hint of rain however and Mam would drag me back inside.

I did have quite a lot of toys: Dinky Cars, Action Man; I tried my best to look after them but whenever little Mikey appeared I'd have to watch in sheer despair as he systematically tried to destroy them. Jigsaws, had a few of those but ultimately they were boring, always insipid outdoor scenes with way too much blue sky or water. Eventually it was Airfix models, I enjoyed the art of assembly, not so much the glueing or painting, but the process of building things was something most young boys enjoyed. We'd build our little dens in the bushes, mess with hay bales out in the fields, and then, whenever we had any snow, we'd practise the art of making igloos, taught by Mr Reeves in school.

I wasn't allowed to roam too far; I felt smothered, rather than mothered. Mam took pride in dressing me up, she liked to call me her 'little soldier.' She was always straightening things, my hair, my clothes, even my posture. "Stand up straight!" she'd snap at me before carefully zipping my anorak up as I stood there holding her lit cigarette.

Meanwhile I was dressed in shorts, even when the other kids weren't. They'd progressed to full-length trousers but Mam was having none of it.

"You'll put on what I tell you to! It's *me* who has to buy your clothes!"

What did *that* mean, shorts were cheap? I'd protest but it was futile.

That was the main theme of my childhood, I was rarely ever told why. When I was it made no sense, I lived in a permanent state of confusion.

"What's the matter with Grandma Busher?"

"What? You wouldn't understand!"

"Why is Uncle Robbie at Nanna's?"

"He's her brother, *isn't* he?"

"But..."

"Shut up! Look, it's none of your business! Go upstairs and read a book!"

I had a curious little mind but rarely got an explanation.

8

So, let's talk about religion. Sometimes we would go to church. Actually, it was a chapel, the Methodist chapel, whatever *that* means. Nanna Peagerm lived close by, my Granda was the maintenance man, always in the boiler room, chopping sticks to feed the fire. I liked it in that boiler room, the heat, the smell, though pretty stifling, when the fire was going full pelt it roared as if it were alive. It almost had a mystical glow, casting shadows against the brickwork, spitting and crackling furiously as wood and coal reduced to ash. Granda always seemed indifferent, it was just a job to him, another pile of logs to split, another fire to set alight. The smoke would sometimes sting my eyes but then I'd just stand back a little, staring deep into the flames, captivated, hypnotised.

My only other brush with religion was the school nativity play, I'd snagged the part of the angel Gabriel, probably because I was tall. They dressed me up in a big white sheet with cardboard wings and a glowing halo, the rest of the cast with makeshift robes that had clearly once been a set of curtains.

I can still remember my lines: *"I bring you tidings of great joy! A king is born to you this day!"* The shepherds with tea towels on their heads. Still, we did seem quite authentic, Jesus was a dark-skinned doll; his mother, Mary, was a virgin. Three wise men? Probably not.

Anyway, the Methodist chapel, my sister went to Sunday School and eventually I was sent there too, like regular school but less informal. We would congregate in the vestry and learn a host of bible stories, what the meaning was behind them wasn't always obvious.

I'd have to ask a lot of questions.

"Why did Jesus talk like that?"

"In parables?"

"Yes, in parables. Some I don't quite understand."

"The Kingdom of Heaven is not for everyone."

"Why?"

"Some prefer to sin."

"Didn't Jesus forgive our sins?"

"Umm . . ."

"Didn't he *die* for them?"

Still, I did enjoy those stories, many made good sense to me, though I was barely seven years old I did feel like a poor, lost sheep. We were encouraged to read the Bible, which came as a shock to me, the loving God seemed terribly angry, not at all like gentle Jesus. He'd destroy entire cities, punish people with a series of plagues, I wondered how many innocent suffered, not everyone deserved such things. And Genesis, that was unreal, it sounded like a fairy story, God waving a magic wand and suddenly everything was created. Men would live for a thousand years, not just one but most, it seemed. Still, I thought, I was just a kid, perhaps that too was some kind of parable?

Then we had to learn a 'piece', a little passage from the Bible, once we'd memorised the thing we'd have to recite it in front of the Minister. Mr Kellows was his name, a powerful man, spoke with authority, he was held in great esteem but the way he seemed to look right through you felt a little strange to me. His steel-grey eyes were often glazy, as if he was close to tears, he had a sallow, haunted look, his mouth, with very narrow lips, seemed somewhat forced, unnatural.

I learned that piece, whatever it was, then at last it was time to recite it, on my own, in front of the Minister, just before the Sunday service. Mrs Dowry led me in, a ghostly figure, very weird, a lot of make-up, angular face, her dark red lips forever pursed as if she was tightly clenching something.

She slid off behind a curtain, everything was suddenly still, the atmosphere felt very strange, it all seemed pretty ominous. I stood there in that holy chamber, all alone, just me and God. The air in there felt very cold, my little hands were trembling. Then at last I detected movement, Mr Kellows strode on in, flowing in his long black robes, almost gliding across the floor but moving with a sense of purpose. He pulled up in front of me and almost half-attempted a smile, then raised his head towards the sky as if he was trying to channel something.

Then he spoke.

"Please begin."

I hesitated for a moment . . . begin what? Oh yes, my piece. I closed my eyes and took a deep breath.

I spoke out loud with the voice of an angel, just like in the nativity play, words echoing all around me, simple stuff but oh-so godly.

Then I was done.

"Yes, my child, you learned that passage beautifully! The Lord and I are very glad."

So was I . . . glad it was over.

Yet, somehow, it wasn't, quite, I felt a hand on top of my brow, a firm, strong hand, fingers parted, startled, I looked straight ahead. His other hand, covered in freckles, made a move towards his garment, gradually, in slow motion, finally it slid inside.

I just stood, completely frozen, scared of what might happen next, I felt constrained, immobilised, like I was stuck in the worst of dreams. Then all of a sudden he whipped it out and waved the damn thing up and down. What on earth was he trying to do? I panicked and made a bolt for it.

I sprinted off towards the door, praying that they'd left it open, if they'd gone and locked the thing I didn't know *what* I was going to do. Thankfully it wasn't locked and I escaped in a matter of seconds. Off I ran, dashing home, sailing on a wind of freedom.

Mam was standing in the kitchen.

"What the hell's the matter with *you?*"

"Not going back there, never, EVER!"

"Whaddya mean?"

"Chapel! None of it!"

Then she gave me the strangest look. "Hey, come on now, tell me what's happened."

"NO, I CAN'T!" I screamed at her.

She would *never* understand.

Still, in time, I spilled my guts and suddenly I began to remember, once, at Granda Busher's house, I'd almost suffered something similar. Mam had sent me up the stairs. "Granda wants to give you something." Up I went, expecting sweets, but what I found was quite unnerving. There he was, sat on the bed, dressed in nothing but a nightshirt. "Hello, Eric, over here!" He had the strangest look on his face. There wasn't any sweets in there, just him, alone, sat on the bed, his bare legs dangling over the edge, it spooked me so I turned and ran.

Then it was the aftermath, a lot of grown-ups got involved, I wasn't any part of it, I didn't really want to be. An argument cropped up at Nanna's, one that really stayed with me. *She* said it was part of life. Instinctively, I knew it wasn't.

"But it's written in the bible: *Suffer the children to come unto me!*"

I'd asked about that very line, in this case, 'suffer' meant 'allow'.

Dad did try and talk to her but she was having none of it. She really thought that kids should suffer.

Right then I was done with religion.

9

Infant school was also done; time to make it as a Junior, there was now a choice to be made though naturally it wasn't mine. The Junior School in Trimley was a tiny old parochial building, far too small for a growing populace, therefore those who couldn't get in were shipped off down the road to Fishwick. There was even a third choice although that was strictly down to religion, Catholics had their own little school on the old back road from Trimley to Colton.

Anyway, I was sent to Fishwick, noted for its stinky coke works, just a five minute ride on the bus, no point kicking up a fuss. Actually, it turned out great, the Fishwick kids seemed cool enough and though the school was pretty old it had its very own indoor pool! The first day seemed a little hectic, everyone was so excited, all those brand new names and faces, could have been daunting, yet it wasn't. I didn't have a chance to be shy as everyone introduced themselves, not formally in front of the teacher but out in the yard at breaks and lunchtime. One by one they made my acquaintance, everyone seemed full of fun, no obvious bullies, which was encouraging, plenty of characters, that's for sure. Chippy Brand, he stood out, a portly lad with a mischievous smile, his party trick was to fold his eyelids and roll his eyes back into his skull. Teddy Charles, a dark-skinned kid, an Afro straight from the

Jackson 5, a non-stop joker, full of himself, I found him very entertaining. Most of the girls were quite nice too, not so much on stage as the boys, softly spoken but really friendly, more so than the Trimley crowd. Occasionally they'd take my hand and lead me to a patch of grass and show me how to make daisy chains or scan the ground for four-leaved clover. It was very curious, I can't say I was captivated, but the presence of the female did seem oddly satisfying. I did have a sister of course but she was four years older than me, the Fishwick girls were more my age, the subtleties seemed very different.

Meanwhile I was a medical marvel, I'd already survived meningitis, not that I remembered much, but around the time I'd started to walk, apparently, I almost died. Struck down fast with flu-like symptoms, almost slipping into a coma, then, amidst a number of tests, they found I had a murmur of sorts, which proved to be a hole in the heart. A scary concept for a kid, which led to annual trips to the hospital, down in Monkton initially, but eventually, as I got older, they sent me to a special unit, further north beyond the Tyne. Professor Julius ran the show, I warmed to him immediately; he'd explain things face to face in a way that I could understand.

"Well, we could close the hole, but *I* don't think that's necessary. Heart surgery has its own risks, but other than *sounding* a little unusual, yours, young man, seems perfectly fine."

He was right about the sound, he loved to test the medical students, one by one they'd hover over me, probing with their stethoscopes.

"How do you think we should proceed?"

"Operate!" was the usual answer.

That was quite concerning at first, but I had full faith in the Professor.

10

Then the pool. What a let down. I was not a natural swimmer. Though I understood the basics somehow I just couldn't grasp it. I had trouble staying afloat while others glided through the water. I was not afraid of it, we simply didn't get along.

There was water all around us, ponds, becks, rivers, the sea; we were told to stay away except for day trips to the beach. TV ads were pretty daunting, warnings from the Grim Reaper, ponds were there to take your soul, mess with those and you'd pay for it. Not that I enjoyed the beach. Deck chairs, crowds, it all seemed pointless, plodging barefoot in the sea, the bloody thing was freezing cold! Even when the weather was hot the sea was having none of it, I much preferred the slot machines, the excitement of the amusement arcade. I'd rush in, shoes full of sand, Dad supplied the 2p pieces, the penny falls had doubled in price since the introduction of decimalisation. It was the skill required that hooked me, timing, vision, some kind of strategy, coins gushing out when you won, allowing you a few more goes.

I was learning fast at Fishwick, Infant School was more a playground, now it seemed that things were structured, proper lessons, different subjects. English, Maths, History, Science, some of it was pretty boring, still, my classmates felt the same so we just sat and lapped it up.

I learned about my limitations, I was not that good at football, though I really loved the game a lot of kids were so much better. It was pretty obvious, the best boys always picked the teams, how quickly they selected you reflected your ability. The standout kid was Peter Lord, he was so much more athletic, sharper, smoother, graceful even, made the beautiful game seem effortless. Being another Trimley lad I got practise with him sometimes, he'd go on to make a professional, no-one was the least surprised.

It seemed I had a musical ear, though music generally hadn't impressed me, most of it was boring and bland, I only liked the quirky combos. Still, one Friday afternoon, they sent me home with a big brass trumpet, God knows why, I didn't choose it, how did they decide such things? It didn't last, for a couple of reasons, first I found it hard to blow, the method involved vibrating your lips, like blowing a raspberry minus the tongue. I struggled with the whole technique, the mouthpiece soon got choked with saliva, that was the kind of mouth I had, I dribbled over everything. The valves and notes I found much easier, I could hardly manage a tune, but I could almost read the music and once I got my lips just right a few stupendous notes were attainable.

"PARP! PARP! P-P-PAAAARRPP!!!"

"BLOODY HELL!" my dad would scream. The whole thing drove him up the wall and pretty soon I was forced to return it.

The other thing I learned at Fishwick was that life just wasn't fair. Reasons why were quite obscure but didn't change the truth of it. A schoolmate died for no good reason, he was such a gentle kid, but just like that, he was gone, it really didn't make much sense. Others would receive abuse, not because of things they did but just because of how they were, things they often couldn't change. Susie Smith with her lazy eye or Teddy Charles with his dusky skin. Not only was it unreasonable but it was cruel and ignorant. The teachers weren't a whole lot better, Mrs James, I used to like her, then one day she punished me for simply screaming out in pain. One of my classmates accidentally slammed a desk lid onto my fingers, my response was 'too extreme' and thus I had my other hand rapped.

11

Then came Spring and new adventures, Dad would take me out on walks, introducing bird nesting, that would be a childhood staple. Mostly it was through the woods, sometimes way across the fields, either way I loved those evenings, it was quality time with Dad, at last, he'd be explaining things. The world of nature, how it worked, stealth, strategy, morals even, things they never taught you at school, I found it so intoxicating. I remember that very first nest, a Whitethroat's down in Howarth Woods, tucked away amongst the brambles, hidden in the undergrowth. The nest was small and fairly scruffy, but the cup was round and deep with five small eggs, grey and speckled, it was just like finding treasure!

"Want one?"

"What?"

"One of the eggs."

"Oooh! Can I?"

"If you're careful."

Turned out there were four strict rules but otherwise it was quite acceptable.

Rule number 1: Take just one, it's all you need, the birds won't miss it. Dad said, on the balance of things, it actually helped the other chicks.

Rule number 2: Don't take any, if you already have that species. Don't take anything you don't need. Duplicates are just being greedy.

Rule number 3: Cover your tracks. Straighten any vegetation.

Rule number 4: Blow the yolk. Otherwise the eggs might rot.

Turned out everyone was at it, almost all the boys I knew; each would have their own collection and loved to show it off to you. Out it came, in a shoebox, lined with sand or cotton wool; sawdust if their dad was a joiner, sometimes simply grass or straw.

And thus, I became an explorer, mostly I'd be off on my own, sometimes in a little group, but then, if you found a nest, you'd always have to break Rule 1. A gang of kids was pretty noisy, nesting did require some stealth, a fluttering bird was often a clue, but only if you got quite close and it only happened if you were silent.

Pre-teen boys were rarely silent. "Moggie off!" a kid would exclaim.

"Where?"

"There, behind that bush!"

Ten minutes later, we'd found nothing.

Still, everywhere had potential, gardens, sheds, garages, trees, the birds would nest in all kinds of places, walls, any kind of construction, even under the eaves of houses. No real need to leave the village, outside it was fraught with danger; farmers, kids from neighbouring villages, not to mention all that water; we had a wealth of gardens and bushes, some patrolled by adults and dogs, however, a nest was always worth it and who could say what else you might find, a tennis ball, an apple tree.

The garages were a favourite haunt, big wooden sheds beyond the bumps, an uneven patch of open ground we had to cross to get to the shops. Robins and blackbirds nested there, not that I didn't have those eggs but finding a nest was a wonderful thing, it proved that you'd developed a skill. The garages were full of all sorts, sometimes you could peer inside, some had grubby little windows, others narrow cracks in the wood where you could get up really close and surreptitiously close one eye. One of them held a vintage car, it looked like it had been abandoned, tufts of grass were blocking the doors, the lock completely covered in rust, the car itself with its grille and headlights buried in a layer of dust.

Farms were always full of potential, there were two in the village itself, one just up around by the church and another looking out over Grangeworth. Stealth was more important here, you wouldn't want the farmer to catch you, still, the rewards were often worth it, pied wagtails, swallows, blue tits, hidden in amongst the livestock.

Livestock, I remember livestock, second time I almost died, a rare excursion out of the village, to "Chats", which was Charity Land. There was a beck and a pond at the bottom, lots of reeds, boggy ground, dangerous enough, I suppose, but it was hard to keep away, the place had such a thriving habitat. Besides the regular coots and moorhens there'd be more exotic species, reed buntings, sedge warblers, possibly things we'd yet to discover. Often you'd see herons there but they'd be breeding somewhere else, our bird books said they nested in colonies, nobody had ever seen one.

There were three of us out that day, me, Steve Robb and Alfie Booker; safety in numbers, you'd have thought, but sometimes three was barely adequate. There we stood in the shallow bog, watching all the cows in the field, docile animals, usually, but we'd been told about a mad one and one of them, stood right at the front, was staring at us, ominously.

"*Just stand still!*" Stevie whispered.

Both my mates were right behind me.

"Just be quiet!" Alfie said.

He didn't understand the concept.

But the cow began to move, slowly at first, then with more purpose, steadily traversing the bog in a beeline for the three of us.

"What do we do? It's coming, it's coming!"

I was getting panicky now, the cow appeared to be getting faster, my instincts were to turn and run.

Guess who else had those same instincts, my companions, Steve and Alfie; they'd already climbed the fence, I couldn't believe I hadn't heard them. Anyway, I turned and ran but in my haste I stumbled slightly, one of my shoes was hanging off having been sucked down in all that mud. I feared the worst, I had no momentum, I could hear a noise behind, I must have made a yard or two and then BANG! Something suddenly hit me. I was face down in the bog. I could hear my two mates screaming. I looked up and saw their faces, fear, guilt, all kinds of emotion. I began to get to my feet. BANG! I was hit again. I'd seen angry bulls before, but this was a cow, lacking horns, weren't they supposed to be fairly amenable? Well, this one surely wasn't. What had made it act this way? I was just a little kid, I wasn't a threat to anybody, least of all a big, fat cow. I just had to get to the fence but now the beast was stood between us, gathering its energy for what I assumed was another attack. And I was right, I wished I was wrong but the damn thing hit me over and over, knocking me onto my back or my belly, depending on which way I was facing. This went on for quite a while until I finally lay there exhausted, that was the strangest thing about it, I'd expected to feel some pain but mostly it was shock and discomfort, laid there in the shallow quag. Then another strange thing happened, my adversary laid on me, its head up against my chest, the weight of it forcing my little body slowly but steadily into the bog. I felt the water up to my ears, this was it, I was actually dying, what a way to go, I thought, but I was certain I was going. Those big, black eyes just stared at me, I stared right back into the abyss. Nothing there had any meaning, everything, it seemed so pointless. But then something curious happened, a wave of fear swept over me, accompanied by a need for survival, something primal had been triggered. Instinctively I went with it and plunged a thumb into one of those eyes, sinking down so very deep that the cow gave out a cry of astonishment, possibly pain, who could tell? And that was it, the thing got up; scrambling up, but it was off me; off it went around in circles, kicking, screaming, quite deranged. A chance, I thought, a final chance! Clearly it was now or never, there was no point trying to think, I simply had to get out of there, fast. With that I found a surge of energy, rolling onto my hands and knees and despite my clothes being utterly drenched I dragged my carcass across to the fence with the beast going totally wild behind me. Climbing it was not an option, I just rolled beneath the wire, my two companions both long gone with no desire to fight a cow. At least they'd gone to fetch my dad who screeched to a halt on a road nearby, the look on his face was quite a picture, not sure if he was worried for me or more for his brand new car's upholstery.

Anyway, I made it at home and Edith Easton ran me a bath, she scrubbed me down from head to toe as Mam got on the phone to the doctor. She was nice, that Edith Easton, dressed in a tight black top and leggings, lovely smile, friendly, pretty, good job I was only eight! The doctor came and examined me. "Nothing's broke that *I* can tell." He said I'd probably have some bruising but all I needed was some rest and before I knew it I'd be fine. Thus I lay there, calm and still, tucked up in my nice warm bed. I guessed I'd had a lucky escape. I closed my eyes and went to sleep.

12

We'd struggled on with decimalisation, 'new money' as everyone called it. Thankfully, as an eight-year old, I'd rarely have to deal with it. Perhaps a trip to the ice cream van. Mr Rossi hated it. "Thruppence," he'd say.
"You mean 3p?"
"I dunno, is so confusing!"
We were engaged with other stuff; bikes, bogeys, marbles, conkers; boys I mean, the girls were different, maybe one or two had bikes. I remember my very first one, hardly dared to ride the thing. When I did I soon fell off. Quite frustrating, embarrassing really. Uncle Ryan soon got wind and slung me down the path one day. Having never used the brakes I ended up in a hawthorn bush.
Marbles caused a bit of trauma, it was like a precursor to gambling, we would beg our mams for them then lose the lot immediately. Mostly to the savvy kids who invented all these stupid rules: spans, blocks, all sorts of things; by the time you followed suit they'd hit you with some other nonsense.
Conkers, what was *that* about? Looking back it seemed so stupid, even collecting them in the autumn, we'd be throwing sticks at trees when there were hundreds laid on the ground. Drilling holes with big, sharp needles, slicing into your own damn flesh, then dangling them on bits of

string before smashing them into your mate's creations, if you were bored, their knuckles instead.

Bogeys were a different artform, dreamed up by the older kids, cobbled together with planks of wood, some pram wheels and a bit of clothes line. There were nuts and bolts involved, some of them were quite elaborate, one of them had actual pedals but can't have been a comfortable ride. Us younger kids were more simplistic in finding ways to propel ourselves, a book on top of a roller skate, or if there was snow, an empty coal sack. We would gather on the bumps in our woolly hats, mitts and wellies, the long, straight path being excellent for hurtling down at incredible speed. Naturally it was dangerous, the uneven slope was pretty steep, but that was always part of the fun, the thrill of risking life and limb or watching some of the smaller kids going arse over tit in their oversized duffle coats.

Next to the bumps we had the rec, a circular field with a road to one side, the village hall perched up at the top and the swings and the slide towards the bottom. We even had a roundabout once but that caused way too many injuries, kids were always being flung off and the council had to scrap the thing. The rec was used for many things, football, cricket, sometimes golf, at one time it was scotch arrows though all you did was throw the things and once you'd mastered that, then what? The annual events were decent, bonfire night, summer carnival, almost everyone would attend, you really felt a sense of community. Jazz bands dominated the carnival, they'd parade around the streets with drums, kazoos, extravagant banners, led by skilful majorettes. They'd toss their batons high in the sky and catch them as they swiftly descended; final judgement came on the field, by which time we'd be bored with it all and laid around in an ice-cream coma.

13

Television seemed competitive, not that we were fully aware of it, still, we were noticing things, the subtle differences between channels. ITV had a show called Magpie, clearly rivalling Blue Peter, a laid back, cooler, hipper version, most of the kids liked one or the other. I was on the fence with both, they seemed to be *telling* you what to do, just like all our teachers and parents, that was not what us kids wanted. It was the BBC in the end who finally put out Why Don't You? A show for kids presented by kids. ITV were sick about that. But hey, it was ITV, too many adverts, even then. The only time they weren't annoying was when they made a funny one or on the lengthy run up to Christmas.

Christmas was a joyful time, it started sometime in November, me and our Judy would ransack the house to find out where they'd hidden the presents. We never did believe in Santa, a fat bloke sliding down the chimney. Millions, in just one night. The thought of it was just plain silly. The day itself was quite predictable, opening presents, feigning surprise, touring some of Dad's relations while Mam got on with the Christmas dinner. We'd return, fully laden, carriers stuffed with selection boxes, Cadbury's, Nestlé, Rowntree's, Mars, enough to see us through the week. Then a scrumptious Christmas dinner, after which we'd watch TV. Classic movies, Christmas specials, few of which we'd watch today. Way before political correctness, things were either funny or not. Why they were or otherwise would take some years to understand. Then more food, turkey sandwiches, dryer than a camel's arse, we'd wash it down with fizzy drinks while gazing at our stash of chocolate. Slumped down on the couch or the floor, watching more inane TV. We'd be allowed to stay up late and watch our parents getting drunk.

After Christmas things seemed dull, it was always cold and depressing. Snow was fun but otherwise it all just seemed so wet and bleak. The trees lacked leaves, the sky lacked colour, a non-stop barrage of wind and rain, so boring, stuck at home or in school, we ached to be out there having fun.

Then one day, a strangely mild one, something happened which would scar me, more than anything I'd experienced, something I could never shake. It happened on a Sunday teatime, Dad was working away from home, a home that always felt quite safe, unfortunately not for much longer. I'd been running around outside, playing football in the street, consequently I was getting hungry and crashed in through the garden gate. I skipped on up towards the door then realised something wasn't right, I heard a commotion in the kitchen, lots of shouting, so unusual, followed by a few sharp screams. Turned out it was Uncle Tom, he was having a fight with mam, struggling, grappling, it was frightening, why's he even here? I thought. He had my mother by the throat, our Judy tugging at her cardigan, both of them looked panic-stricken, I just stood there petrified.

"STOP IT!!!" I screamed, "GERROFF!!! GERROFF!!!"

Uncle Tom just snarled at me. Next I knew his fist came out and knocked me to the kitchen floor. I sat there stunned. What was happening? Yes, he was an ugly git, but violent? This was news to me. Clearly he was very drunk as the whole room stank of alcohol.

The fight continued, it was horrible; momentarily Mam broke free, at least from the death-grip on her neck, but the whole ordeal was far from over. "LEAVE ME ALONE, YOU FILTHY PIG!!!" Uncle Tom just started growling; then he lunged at her again. "GET OFF, YOU BASTARD!!! USE THE KIDS!!!"

Wait . . . WHAT? Use the *KIDS?* I was stunned to say the least, I went from being shocked and scared to mortified in a matter of seconds. Use us for what? Didn't matter, nobody was using *me*, I scrambled up and legged it out of there, sprinting off into the distance.

I just ran and ran and ran, no idea where I was headed, ending up at the edge of the village, staring off across the fields. I was stood at a barbed wire fence, I thought of climbing it and continuing but it was slowly getting dark and the distant woods seemed quite foreboding. What could I do? Where could I go? Nanna's? No! *She* wouldn't care. *She* thought little kids should suffer, as far as *I* knew, *everyone* did. But *my mother?* That was upsetting. OK, she was being abused, but offering her *kids* instead? That was almost unforgivable.

I just couldn't work it out. What was Uncle Tom demanding? Something sexual, I guessed, but I hardly knew what sexual was. The whole thing was a mystery, some kissing and cuddling was involved, then something else to do with your bits, as Granda Busher, Mr Kellows, both of them had their todgers out. But what came next I hadn't a clue. Who knew *what* they were trying to do? It frightened me and terrified Mam, I'd never seen such a look on her face. Our Judy too, it was scary, I couldn't bear to think about it, Mam was clearly terrified but her response was so disturbing. Weren't your parents supposed to love you? Weren't they supposed to *care* for you? We were fed and clothed and housed yet suddenly it counted for nothing. What about a bit of protection? Where was Dad when we needed him? Did other kids have to go through this? Weren't we all supposed to be *family?*

It was pretty hard to take, I don't remember going back but obviously I did in the end, by which time things had calmed a little. It was never spoken of. It was like it never happened. Dad came back eventually and life continued on as normal. What I do remember however was sitting alone on a cold, brick wall, full of emotion, anger, frustration, tears streaming down my face. Then all of a sudden I started screaming, screaming at the sky above. "WHY? WHY? WHY AM I HERE? Part of me just didn't belong. True, I was born on earth but something inside seemed otherworldly, what could it be, my spirit perhaps? I couldn't conceive of anything else. I'd felt it long ago in my bedroom, leaving my body and drifting away, unable to settle, ever restless, was my soul reluctant to stay? Maybe life on earth was a punishment, maybe God *was* always angry, I'd already rejected religion but that didn't mean he didn't exist. I wanted him to answer me, I needed it, demanded it, important things were never explained, not by God or *anybody*.

I just sat there sobbing away. Why did bad things have to happen? If it was simply Uncle Tom perhaps I could have coped with it. Mam and Dad had given me plenty. How come it was never enough? Forgiveness would be a long time coming. Understanding even longer.

14

Back at school, things were changing, suddenly we were being judged. Tests, report cards, there were standards, things took on a serious tone. I did well with most of the tests, mainly due to paying attention, some of the other kids struggled a bit but that only seemed to bother the teachers. Report cards, they were something else, the negatives would peeve me a little. Was that really me, I wondered. Someone clearly thought it was.

"Eric is an intelligent lad with skill in academic work but needs a firm hand to bring out his best, otherwise his work can be sloppy."

So? That stuff hardly mattered. There weren't *any* perfect kids and most of the adults were sadly lacking so all in all I did OK.

That particular summer was poor, dry but cool, not much sun. Mam had a job at the clothing factory, much of the time we spent at Nanna's. We were not allowed to stray, while other kids were off on adventures, we'd be forced to stay indoors, killing time with books or board games, sometimes sneaking into the garden. Places developed a mystical quality, none more so than the 'three beechies', a quite distinct collection of trees a couple of fields away in the distance. Kids would flock and make a rope swing, angering the local farmer; it seemed like a dangerous place but I would dream of being there.

Then we'd stay at Auntie Maisie's, there we'd have a sense of freedom, no restrictions, in or out, at least none that we ever adhered to. "Don't go far!" she'd say half-heartedly, probably glad to see the back of us, next I knew, her Mikey Boy would drag me off to somewhere distant.

We'd meet other kids on the way. "Who the hell is this?" they'd ask.

"It's me cousin," he'd reply. "He's from Trimley."

"We HATE Trimley!"

Then I discovered I hated heights. Mikey dragged me off to the quarry. There we stood, right on the edge, I felt quite sick, disorientated. Next a family trip to Blackpool, which involved a trip up the tower. How exciting, I was told. I almost shat myself up there. I ended up on the viewing gantry, it was cold and extremely windy and as I was looking out through the bars I suddenly felt incredibly vulnerable. I held on for dear life, my stomach felt so tight and queasy, I could not look up or down, I had to gaze off into the distance. That was not so pleasant either, I was forced to close my eyes, but any relief was not forthcoming; lacking any visual stimuli, my imagination took over, daylight plunging into dark as I plummeted to an early death.

15

The rest of the year was uneventful, something about a pregnancy, my folks were more concerned than me, I'd deal with it when the big day came. I got Subbuteo for Christmas, what a load of crap *that* was, a ball that almost dwarfed the players. Utterly ridiculous!

Then came 1973, which started with a bang, a *big* one, a lorry skidded out at a junction and slammed right into our old school bus. That was pretty harrowing, seeing the driver dead on the road, us kids were only bumped and bruised but life seemed so precarious.

Occasionally I was home alone, parents working, sister elsewhere, I did have lots of books and toys but found it hard to concentrate. Things were suddenly bothering me, not specific things, just everything, so many thoughts oppressing my mind, it felt like I was losing it. I'd make up all these silly games, like kicking around a rolled-up sock, I'd have some target or goal in mind and if it took fifteen kicks to make it I wouldn't be able to stop repeating it till I could do the same in ten. Then I'd try my hand at Patience, that was quite addictive too, those cards were just a bunch of numbers but if the numbers didn't align I couldn't stop until they did. I wanted to, I *needed* to, the urge was almost overwhelming, it even pervaded simple tasks like turning a light switch on or off a specific number of useless times.

Then, in March, my brother was born; Martin was his given name, everyone was so excited, I guessed that I was pleased for them. I didn't really know what to make of it, suddenly I had a brother, but I was a whopping nine years older, I couldn't decide if it was a positive. That all changed when they brought him home, he seemed so tiny and delicate, not only was he brand new life but this little kid was part of a family. Though I knew that mine was fucked and people generally couldn't be trusted, I was fed and clothed and housed, I *had* to believe that it meant something. I had a sister who nurtured me, we rarely argued, that was great, and now we had a little brother, we needed to look after him. I'd watch him as he slept in his cot, his chest gently undulating, he looked oh-so small and fragile, I was scared to pick him up. Once, he didn't seem to be breathing, off I ran to raise the alarm. Of course, there was nothing wrong with him, like most things it was all in my mind. Still, I felt the need to protect him, this world wasn't safe for kids. We were all so weak and vulnerable, grown-ups couldn't always save you. I would have to watch him carefully, make sure he was never alone, I never felt I had much worth but maybe this was a turning point?

Then we got a colour TV, it was one of the strangest things, we viewed the outside world with colour but seeing it on the TV screen felt suddenly rather magical. It breathed new life into everything, the programmes suddenly seemed so real, but *more* real, it was really weird, our lives, it seemed, were changing, fast.

The final of the FA Cup. Me and Dad and Judy watched it; one of the local teams were playing, Sunderland, the underdogs. They'd made it from Division 2, chances were they'd end up slaughtered, still, it was quite an achievement and there was sure to be lots of goals.

Wrong, there was only one, but it was scored by Sunderland and the moment the ball hit the back of the net my dad leapt up from his seat and screamed as if he'd scored the damn thing himself. Me and our Judy sat in amazement, rarely did he show emotion, not only that, we'd had the impression he wasn't a fan of *any* team. He'd taken us to matches before; Middlesbrough, Hartlepool, even Ipswich; Auntie May lived quite close by and Uncle Seth was a regular there, despite the fact they'd signed a darkie. Sunderland? Perhaps a few but never had he got excited, we thought he was neutral but they proved to be his childhood team.

After that he took us often, there was a special coach from Trimley, if he wasn't working away, we'd all have fish and chips for lunch then off we'd trot across the bumps to the beige and brown of Bobberty's bus. I loved those days, the feel of the crowd, thousands of people cheering as one, you really felt a part of something, your heart beat faster, it was magic! We'd be stood in the Paddock End, wrapped up in our scarves and hats, looking forward to half-time Bovril, possibly a bag of nuts. Of course, it was Division 2 and you had to learn to cope with defeat. That didn't seem to bother Dad. "The club don't pay *my* wages," he said.

16

Then, two years down at Fishwick, local education changed, a shake-up of the schools was in order and pretty much everyone was affected. The kids who went to the secondary school were suddenly bundled off to Sedgeworth; their old school became the juniors, lots of room for everyone. The whole of the parochial school, the Trimley kids who'd missed the cut. Everybody was invited, though not everyone accepted. Peter Lord remained at Fishwick, maybe he was happy there? I was to a certain extent, but what was the point of catching a bus and risking yet another crash?

So, back to a local school, down in the corner of the village, just past Nanna's, a modern building, drab, rectangular, featureless. There was however a good-sized field, a playground and a gym at the back, there wasn't any sign of a pool but who liked swimming anyway?

Most of the kids I knew of course, from the Infants, Fishwick or out in the street; the teachers seemed a little strange but given time to settle in I guessed that I'd get used to them. We made good use of that big, old field, non-stop football, jumpers for goalposts, till that is, one sunny lunchtime, I was being diplomatic and made the mistake of going in goal. I wasn't a keeper in any sense, I couldn't dive or jump that well, my arms though long enough were clumsy, most of my saves were done with my feet. It was instinct, an outfield player, goalies could get kicked in the head; diving at someone's feet seemed stupid, why not use your legs instead? And so I did. Big mistake. Lesley Beanson had the ball, a stocky-looking, powerful brute, perhaps he should have been in goal? Anyway, I slid towards him, made good contact with the ball, unfortunately Lesley didn't and his big boot smashed into my shin.

"AYAAAAAH!!!" rang out through the crowd.

Big Les laughed. "Sorry, mate!"

Didn't look like he was sorry. He looked rather proud of himself.

I was shipped off to the nurse, quite surprised we actually had one. Maybe it was a dinner lady, can't remember, I was in pain!

"It doesn't look too bad," she said, "you'll no doubt have a lot of bruising." She applied a little bandage and then, when the bell rang out, she sent me hobbling back to class.

The teacher didn't give a damn. "Blummin' heck, it's Hopalong Cassidy!" Mr Whale, a right old git. Curly ginger hair and glasses. Couldn't put any weight on the leg, the right one, it was way too painful, all I could do was stand on the left, so that old scumbag and most of the class proceeded to embarrass me. He was good at taking the piss. Cruel, but no-one seemed to care. Everyone just laughed along, as long as they weren't the butt of his jokes it was pointless contradicting him. I laughed one time and he screamed at me.

"LOOK AT HIM! LOOK AT HIM! HE LOOKS LIKE *EMU* FROM TV!"

I could never live *that* down.

I'll always remember the colour blind tests. They were done as a group, in class.

"Who sees number 37?"

A show of hands.

"Right, stand up!"

There were three of us, all of us boys.

"YOU, my friends, are COLOUR BLIND!"

The rest of the class all sat there laughing.

Thanks, Mr Whale.

What a twat.

The other thing he liked to do was make us go sit next to Mandy, a skinny, fairly backward girl who liked to stick things up her nostrils.

When somebody misbehaved it was, "RIGHT! OVER THERE WITH MANDY!"

Not quite sure how Mandy felt but she would never seem to complain.

Anyway, the day was done, my poor leg wasn't any better, I did try to hop on home but soon collapsed through sheer exhaustion. Someone went for Granda P. who carried me most of the way on his back; the Doctor was called, then an ambulance; off I went to hospital.

An X-ray later, it was confirmed: a hairline fracture of the tibia, came home with a pot on my leg, I got more attention than the baby! Two of my classmates paid me a visit, on their way to school next day. Should've seen the look on their faces. Not a softie after all!

Then the doctor popped back in.

"Hmm," he said, "I don't like that! Not another Jamie Bainbridge!"

Right away I knew what he meant.

Jamie was a hopalong too, but his condition seemed to be permanent, he had also broken a leg, but *his* pot hadn't set quite right and as a result he walked with a limp as if one leg didn't match the other.

Off I went, back to hospital, one of the doctors seemed to agree, my pot was not in the right position and as a result of this aberration, out they came with a pair of bolt croppers!

Anyway, I made it home and everyone wrote on my brand new pot. Tradition, see, but what the hell, at least I had some company. It wasn't easy moving around, especially when it was toilet time, a bedpan and bottle, what a fuss, and I read my books a dozen times.

Then one day I had a visitor, silvery hair, a knot on his eye, a personal tutor, it transpired, the school didn't want me left behind. That was very nice of them, a guilty conscience or standard practice? Well, whatever, here we were, it wasn't as if I had a choice.

But he was great, that nice old tutor, had a twinkle in his eye, he talked to me, he actually *talked*, explaining things in such great detail. He would whizz through maths and science. "How'd you work that out?" he'd say. I'd tell him. "Ah, a logical lad!" He saw patterns in my brain.

When it came to other subjects he would ask me what I thought. History, say.

"Well, it's boring, how can I remember it all?"

"Right. All those dates and facts?"
"Yeah."
"OK, this might help. First, think of it as stories. You like stories?"
"Yes, I do."
"Think of everyone as characters, history's just a bunch of stories, picture the characters in your mind, doing all the things they did."
"What about dates?"
"Make connections, like the old Columbus rhyme."
"Fourteen-hundred and ninety-two?"
"Right! Make some up of your own."

He was full of stuff like that, we romped through everything from school, and more, things I'd come across later, home tuition made such a difference.

After that, school was easy, I was now ahead of the class. So what if Mr Whale was a bastard? I'd get through it all despite him.

I was protective of the leg, my muscles were weak, it took some time; even when I resumed playing football I still seemed rather hesitant. My left became the leg of choice, so strange, I was used to my right, but somehow it rewired my brain, in the long term it was an absolute godsend. There I was, a two-footed player, I even got a school team trial, I wasn't exactly ready for it but I was thankful for the experience. Most of the older kids were supportive, great, I thought, a proper team. Perhaps next year, the coach suggested. Fair enough. I could wait.

17

Power cuts. They were something. No-one seemed to know quite why, but there we were, surrounded by candles, it was like the Middle Ages. It was pretty spooky at first but then you had to face reality. Wasn't *that* much you could do. Grab a torch and pretend to be Mysterons.

I was fond of kids TV, watching all that stuff with our Martin; not so scary anymore, but still, lots of talking animals. Some of them imaginary, The Wombles, oh he loved that show, he'd sit there in his romper suit, trying his best to sing the theme tune.

Then one day the shows arrived, a regular army of travelling folk, who brought a fairground to the bumps, infusing them with a splash of colour. Sideshows, lights, stalls, rides; we'd be begging our parents for cash and come back with a sad little goldfish, destined to die in a week or two.

I noticed a wire to the Bevans's house.

"What's *that* for?" I had to ask.

Apparently for power to the caravans, they'd been offered a ten pound note.

"Don't they have generators for that?"

Mr Bevans looked at me. One eye this way, one eye that, I decided not to pursue the matter.

The final year of junior school was memorable to say the least, music now appealed to me, I became a fan of Top of the Pops! Glam rock, I loved all that; fun, colourful, energetic, our Judy even dressed the part and went to school in glitter make-up! There were lots of records downstairs, most of them were pretty boring, except for one, a compilation, quite eclectic for my parents. There was one song, 'Voodoo Chile', it captured my imagination, wild, intense, screeching guitar; surprised that 'Chile' was not the country, didn't quite know *what* it was. I do know I was noticing girls, not in any sexual way, but some of those sleeves were quite appealing, even though I didn't know why. There was one girl back at school, Mary-Anne Weathers, she intrigued me; bright, funny, talented, pretty, I suddenly felt intimidated. Long, black hair, big, brown eyes, deep, evocative, captivating, her dad had something to do with the church, but I could hardly hold *that* against her. She could really play the piano, a prodigy by all accounts, she pushed me at the top of the class though I was there reluctantly.

Pressure came from somewhere else, one or two of the girls had boyfriends, something most of us boys looked down upon, still, occasionally it happened. I remember an actual marriage, a fake one, but it was entertaining, it did seem weird for ten-year old kids but the bride and groom seemed pretty happy.

"You're next!" one of my schoolmates said.

"Whaddya mean?"

"Mary-Anne!"

"Rubbish!" I said. I liked the girl but marriage was simply out of the question.

Then came casting for a play. "Bill and Lill," I seem to recall. A school play, to be performed in public, guess who they wanted to play the leads? Mary-Anne was very pleased, reluctantly I went along, as a kid I was still quite shy and the thought of reciting lines on stage, in front of an audience, terrified me. But still, it was more than that, I realised it immediately, as soon as Mary-Anne started to speak I was almost helpless, totally dumbstruck. She'd a husky, passionate voice, an artist, an actress, naturally. I could barely read my lines. I stuttered, yes, I actually stuttered!

In the end I became the narrator, getting laughs at the very first show, reciting the intro with aplomb then failing to find the gap in the curtains. Mary-Anne disappeared soon after, I was told she'd moved away. God had called her dad down south, I somehow thought he'd done me a favour.

I did make the football team, left-half my assigned position, we were solid, had some flair, not me, but my strong left foot was quite an asset playing there. Yellow shirts and socks, black shorts, screw-in studs were now in vogue, it made it easy to clean your boots, though moulded studs were still alright since long before you wore them down you'd suddenly need the next size up. We finished second in everything, the league itself and both the cups; two of them were won by Fishwick, mostly down to Peter Lord. Some of those games were pretty spicy, villages back then were hostile; tribal, insular, often violent, even at our tender age. The bus got bricked on a trip to Hasforth, what we deserved for winning one-nil. If we'd lost we'd have got the same, it was like the old wild west, with kids!

The nesting season was intense, we really ventured out and explored, mostly in a little gang, as miles away on the old back roads it really wasn't safe on your own. A favourite haunt was Crystal Canyon, an ancient quarry close to Kelton, that too had a mystical quality, which evolved as you got older. First time there I went with Dad, he showed me all these shiny crystals, quartz, he said, little value, still, I had a fertile mindset, how did *he* know they weren't real diamonds? Then we played around with echoes, we'd experiment with our voices, changing tone, volume, pitch, those rocky walls were fascinating.

"COO! COO!"

"EY-O! EY-O!"

"BIG DOG'S COCKS!"

The sound of laughter.

Finally, the silence got you. When you stood there all alone you could almost feel it in your bones, a stark and chilling atmosphere, echoes of events of yore, some of which felt quite disturbing.

As for nests, they were varied, jackdaws up among the cliffs, wrens and wagtails lower down, thrushes in amongst the bushes. Way beyond, lots of woodland, hawks, jays, various owls, it stretched along to the modern quarry, Gammy, on the edge of Kelton.

Then there was the Foxy, (the Fox Covert), Granda called it Pogles Wood, we rarely found any nests in there but woods were always so much fun and the Foxy was by far the closest, just past Chats which I still explored, providing there weren't any cows in the field.

Further east we had The Res, bordering on Howarth Woods; ducks, geese, swans, waders, dozens of species gathered there. Braver kids would go for a swim, it didn't look too safe to me, but it was miles away from humanity so perhaps it *was* quite clean.

Fishwick Moors, the Whinney Banks, we were surrounded by natural beauty, Wynston Woods beyond Carr's pond, the old lost village of Emblesworth. The hours I whiled away out there, exploring, detecting, discovering things, a growing collection of marvellous eggs, tucked away beneath my bed. At night, I would scour my bird books, looking for species I didn't have and wondering how I might acquire them, some seemed way beyond my reach. Guillemot, Razorbill, Cormorant, Shag, I could never scale a cliff. Goshawk, Buzzard, Golden Eagle, imagine your hand in one of *those* nests, the birds would tear it into pieces! I was jealous of other kids, some collections were impressive, Tony Donahue, for example, he had eggs from mainland Europe. Night Heron, Pin-tailed Sand Grouse, where the hell did *they* come from? Inherited from his uncle, he said, but wasn't he just a local poacher who rarely strayed too far from home? Some of those eggs had fancy writing, names inscribed with a delicate pen, to me they looked like museum pieces, I guessed that once they probably *had* been. Little Mikey had some luck, his dad had driven him up on the moors and came back with a carful of eggs, gulls, curlews, grouse, plovers. Good job *my* dad worked away, now and then he'd return with something, an oystercatcher's egg one day, he'd found the nest at the side of the road.

Luck was one thing, skill another, I do remember one day after tea, beyond the back road, west of Grangeworth, stood in a stretch of patchy scrub which I thought had shown a lot of promise. A small bird fluttered out from the grass, a warbler perhaps, maybe a pipit, it was often hard to tell, all you'd see was a flash of something, mostly a subtle shade of brown. Anyway, I started searching, not a thing, no sign of a nest, the bird may well have just been feeding but it was the height of the breeding season, surely there was *something* there. Think, Eric, think. What do I do? Patience was the obvious answer, thus I withdrew to the side of the road and plonked myself down on the grassy verge.

There I sat, completely still, staring at the vegetation, it felt like I was meditating, senses melding into one. Not quite sure how long I waited, minutes probably, felt like hours, all I know is I was certain that if there *was* a nest out there that little bird, shy as it may have been, sooner or later would have to return. And, at last, it finally did, preceded by the strangest feeling that something was out there, hidden, approaching, even though there was nothing moving. There was not the slightest sound, seconds later, there it was, that tiny bird, oh-so dainty, perching on a swaying stalk before gently dropping to the ground.

I sat there for a few more minutes, focussed like an apex predator, eyes fixed on the very same spot the little bird had fallen into. This is how it's done, I thought. Stealth, strategy, guile, persistence. I'd been sitting there like a statue, backside getting damp from the grass but hardly daring to change position.

Finally I made my move, as slowly and silently as I could; softly, carefully, gently creeping, hardly even daring to blink. I was steadily closing in, just a few more feet, I pleaded. Not yet little bird, not yet, then all of a sudden, off it went.

Right, I thought, I've got it now; still, it took an age to find it, such a tiny, magical nest, woven from the finest grass stems and camouflaged impeccably. Five small eggs, finely specked, it was hard to take just one but I followed the rules, obediently, and with that in mind I set off home, feeling rather pleased with myself.

The books came out. There it was: Grasshopper Warbler, the pictures matched, the bird, the nest, the eggs, the habitat, even the softly skulking behaviour. It felt great, the skill, the patience, I had earned this fine reward. None of my friends had such an egg, I'd have to keep the location secret.

18

Then the end of junior school, my last report was fairly typical. Excellent work but a tad untidy, that was a constant theme throughout. I didn't care about such things, I had no desire to be perfect, everyone was lacking something, why not focus on the good?

The holidays were pretty strange, they had an air of impending doom as Sedgeworth Comprehensive was next and all we heard were horror stories. First year kids were terrorised, we'd be bullied by older kids, we'd have our heads stuffed down the toilet, stuff like that, it was harrowing. The reality was such a relief, we hardly mixed with older kids; everything was new and exciting, no-one gave us any trouble. Who'd invented all those stories, were they all just winding us up? Anyway, for the moment at least, the signs were looking pretty good.

Three school buses ferried us in, scooping us up from the nearby villages, one for the girls, one for the boys and a coach, mixed, for those who preferred it. We'd assemble at the library, not knowing which would turn up first, the coach was much more comfortable but the other buses, such as they were, were infinitely more appealing. Double deckers, both of them, our bus was as noisy as the passengers, older boys would sit upstairs, terrorising the steward, Charlie. They would stand and rock the thing, quite violently, from side to side and then when Charlie came to chastise them, he'd be pelted with scrunched up paper and taunted with the same old tune:

Charlie had a pigeon, a pigeon, a pigeon
Charlie had a pigeon, a pigeon he had
It flew in the morning, it flew in the night
And when it came home it was covered in
Shhaaarlie had a pigeon, a pigeon, a pigeon
Charlie had a pigeon, a pigeon he had . . .

Not the most original song but we sang it all the way to Sedgeworth.

It was quite an imposing school, reminding me of an ocean liner, the bulk of it four storeys high with two big chimneys up on top. Surrounding it were smaller buildings, the science block, the dining hall, the gym and the assembly hall, it took a bit of getting used to.

We were assigned to form 1-H. That was mostly Trimley boys, a few from Sedgeworth, or elsewhere, the girls were mostly from Bishop Middleton. Some of the boys spoke proper English, middle class I guess you'd say. Their mums and dads had better jobs, they lived on some of the newer estates.

Lessons were strictly regimented, teachers all had expertise. Single half-hour periods or doubles, laid out neatly in a table. Maths was taught by Mr Handson, Henson would have been more apt, he had the look of a weird old muppet, straggly hair, John Lennon glasses, moustache springing in all directions. English, that was Mr Laine, a fop, a dandy, full of culture; Jason King but much more blonde, you felt he needed a drink in his hand. History was Mr Rollinson, military through and through, a wooden arm, down to some battle, he would use it on occasion. Science was now split into three, Biology, I did like that, with Mr Mawson, spoke with authority, clear, concise, which I respected. Fulsome mop of ginger hair, a thick moustache but his was neat, he wouldn't stand for any nonsense, some of his put-downs were spectacular. Physics was a different story, all those forces and equations, none of which seemed tangible, it was like the very worst part of Maths. Mr Stantley ran the show, dour and serious, like the subject, he'd attempt to liven it up, but it was Physics, not a chance. Chemistry, now there's a subject, that was full of equations too but you could see it demonstrated, often quite explosively. Mr Darnston was the teacher, he looked fairly neat but wild, bulging eyes, quite disturbing, could have been a maniac. "Overactive thyroid," he said, "relax, I'm not gonna kill you; more chance of you killing yourself, the chemistry lab is a dangerous place!" He'd proceed to show us why, those Bunsen burners were bad enough but the power and force of some reactions were bordering on insanity. Hydrogen rockets, sodium particles, buzzing around a beaker of water, cornflour bombs, phosphorus flames, I loved it, it was so dramatic.

Didn't like the uniform, black and grey, a splash of white. Everybody looked the same, indeed, the very point of it. Girls back then were forced to wear skirts, didn't bother us at the time, but when the weather was freezing cold it was difficult not to see the injustice.

Morning assembly, hated that, all those speeches by the teachers, then those bloody awful hymns, I could hardly sing a note. We would stand there in a line, some of us mouthing silently, a couple making silly changes, heathens we were, the lot of us!

Breaks were brief, except at lunchtimes, you could choose the dining hall or escape to the village if so desired; just because you had dinner money it didn't mean you were forced to buy tickets. Though school meals were cracking value and sometimes you'd be offered seconds, you could hold on tight to the cash and blow the lot on sweets and crisps.

If it was dry we'd hit the field, mostly kicking a ball around, jumpers down occasionally but mostly we would use our bags and there were goalposts on the big pitch. Peter Vardy hated this, he seemed to lack coordination, by the time he'd aimed a kick the ball would have eluded him. Thus he invented a brand new game, 'foulogomai' he liked to call it; out would come a plain white golf ball, after which a riot ensued. The object wasn't to kick the thing but pretend to in creative ways, while forcefully kicking each other instead, the whole thing was completely insane! Still, it was lots of fun, like judo and football rolled into one, bodies strewn across the floor, the Sedgeworth kids could hardly believe it. "What the hell have *you* been doing?" our teachers would ask in the afternoons, we'd sit there in our grass-stained clothes, bedraggled, scruffy, sweating profusely. We'd be grinning like imbeciles, occasionally we'd try to explain it. Blank expressions in return. Trimley boys were *very* strange.

Real school fights were quite an event, they'd happen after the final bell, as everyone crossed the field to the buses, "FIGHT!" would ring out from the throng and a mass of bodies would converge, a five-deep circle of rabid kids with two protagonists at the centre. First you'd find out who they were, then you'd have to pick a side; if you could you'd cheer for them, if not you'd just enjoy the spectacle, glad it wasn't you involved. I got sick of them in the end, some of those fights were pretty brutal, blood exploding all over the place, nobody was solving anything. They were always broken up, often by an angry teacher, tossing us all aside with impunity, screaming how stupid violence was.

Hypocrisy was everywhere, those teachers were as bad as our parents. "Do as I say, not as I do!" You couldn't teach a thing like that. Mr Blatt, a science teacher, he was one of the best examples, a big, round bloke, bespectacled, but if he caught you talking in class he'd launch a blackboard rubber at you with little regard for health and safety. Didn't care if he took an eye out; answer him back? Big mistake. He wouldn't send you off to the office, he'd just fetch his own damn cane and give you a thrashing in front of the class.

19

Then, things began to change. First thing was unusual language. Words I didn't understand: spunk, tampax, stuff like that. What the hell were they on about? I laughed along with everyone else. Did *anybody* know, I wondered. Things like that would bother me.

At home, Dad was acting weird, he'd been like this for some time now, it started with the hairpin thing, the first time he'd been cruel to me. He said I had a blackhead problem, claimed I hadn't been washing my face, I knew I had but he wouldn't listen and led me sternly into the bathroom where he suddenly clamped my head and dug them out while I just stood there, helpless, mystified, forced to endure it. Next he took me out one night, to a house just down from Nanna's; said he had some plans to assess but what did it have to do with *me?* A bald little fellow answered the door; I was sent upstairs with his daughter, Lorna, she was around my age, remembered her from Junior school. Lorna was a nice-looking girl, slender, blonde hair down to her shoulders, had a pleasant disposition but why the hell was I there in her bedroom? It felt weird, very strange, the room was full of girly things, posters, pillows, cuddly toys, she'd show me something. "Nice," I'd say. I simply wasn't interested, what was I supposed to say? She had a peculiar look on her face. I smiled and walked across to the window.

Lorna joined me.

"Whaddya see?"

"Oh, just people, walking about."

It was only six o'clock but already it was getting dark.

"I know him," she said.

"Who?"

"Him there, the one with the dirty-looking jacket. He's not nice."

"Most folks aren't."

"I know," she said, "I know what you mean."

Then more strangeness in the bathroom, Dad insisted I cleansed my foreskin.

"Why?"

"You might end up like me, they had to have me circumcised."

He explained the gory details.

Ugh, I thought. Not for me. From that point on I did as he said, my private parts were delicate.

So delicate, one night they exploded; I leapt out of bed in a panic. I was suddenly terribly sore, pyjamas wet, oh God, I was bleeding! What had happened? What was wrong? I hardly dared to look down there. When I finally did, no blood, instead a creamy, sticky mess.

My mother looked quite unconcerned as she met me at the bedroom door. "Take those bottoms off," she told me. "Then go clean up in the bathroom."

So I did. Trouble was, soap and water didn't help, my willie suddenly started to grow, much longer, harder, it was inflating! Though quite sore and very tender, there was a kind of tingling there, not pain, at least not pain as I knew it, this was clearly something new.

Of course, soon the penny dropped, at last I realised what had happened. I was now a sexual being; I was slowly becoming a man. My willie? Couldn't leave it alone. Must have filled a thousand socks. Tissues simply weren't enough, I was now an unstoppable sperm machine!

There was a Sex Ed talk at school, the whole class sat there sniggering, the language used seemed very formal but since I was going through all that stuff the practicalities did make sense. Unfortunately there were other changes, the rest of my body was growing too, my legs, my face were getting longer, hair was sprouting up all over. I was changing, girls were changing, they were developing breasts and hips, I looked at them in a different way, all of a sudden I found them attractive. Somebody had flipped a switch, it all seemed very strange and new, my voice broke, I had seen it in others but when it happens to you it's madness.

Then the cruellest joke of nature. Acne. Great volcanoes of it. Just as the girls were becoming attractive I was now a hideous beast. I could barely look at myself, my own reflection made me sick, the hairpin treatment hadn't helped, I soon found out that nothing would, not squeezing or spot cream, it was useless. Squeezing was messy and often painful, it would lead to scabs and scars, the creams and lotions, utterly pointless, however you attacked the thing it all came rushing back with a vengeance. I could hardly look at a girl, it was easier to ignore them, school meant interacting of course, but it was tough without any confidence. Others had it, some much worse, but *that* didn't help, not one iota, it was hard to look at them and that meant others felt the same if they were forced to look at me. The ones that weren't affected? Bastards. How could anyone have it so easy, the beautiful ones, the confident ones, injustice wasn't confined to the girls.

It was torture after that, I couldn't stand for anything much, in each and every situation, all I saw were negatives. Not that some of them weren't real, our P.E. teachers, they were wankers, if it rained on P.E. day it only meant one thing: Cross Country. Sedgeworth was surrounded by countryside, farms, fields, gently rolling; off we'd go on a five mile run and should we fail to get back on time we'd only be losing our lunchtime break. Those P.E. teachers were lazy swines, both were quite surprisingly fat, contented, smug and slightly sadistic, everybody grew to despise them. One of them would act so cool, smoked a pipe, sang in a folk band, tried to be friendly while taking the piss, I really hated folks like that.

The girls had quite a slender mistress, short hair, blonde, a little stuffy; never ever seemed to smile but always spoke with perfect English.

No-one seemed to like her much.

"Isn't she nice?"

"Yeah, *too* nice!"

"*Too* nice? But she never smiles!"

"Oh, you lads, you never get it!"

Well, *I* didn't, that's for sure; one of those runs was fairly typical, off we trotted into the rain, boys *and* girls, everyone equal. It was like a long line of misery, single file, forever stretching, fastest runners way up front, the rest of us stringing out behind. The rain came down, harder and harder, laughing at us, soaking our kit, the end result we carried more weight; it was nothing less than discouraging. Some took shelter under a tree but most of them had lost their leaves and standing around was no real help, not when your lunch break was at stake.

I soldiered on, sick and disheartened, shuffling up the muddy tracks, Robinson's farm was next en route, surely the farmer wasn't too pleased with scores of schoolkids, spotty and sweaty, traipsing through his farm each day? Anyway, there was a little shed, I noticed two of the girls in there; Debbie McKaye and Angela Big Tits, not sure what her real name was.

"Eric! Over here!" yelled Debbie.

She was nice, lovely smile, I got the feeling she liked me a little but what did it matter, I was a mess, I didn't even like myself.

Nevertheless I bounded over.

"Come on, ladies, make some room!"

Angela frowned and pushed me aside.

"Keep your hands to yourself, young man!"

Young man? I was in their class! Obviously, I *was* quite young but she spoke to me like an errant child, she sounded more like one of the teachers. She was tall, as tall as me, a mop of tight, black, curly hair; big, full lips, insane blue eyes, her chest was ample, naturally, but so were her thighs, quite thick and muscular, she could do some damage with those.

"So, what now?" I asked them, smiling.

"Nowt!" said Angela. "Nothing at all!"
I looked at Debbie. "Whaddya think?"
"I dunno, I'm just so *cold!*"
Grab her, I thought. Give her a cuddle!

Thinking didn't achieve a damn thing, that Angela Big Tits beat me to it and off she ran with Debbie in tow, buttocks jiggling through the farmyard.

20

The next two years were much the same, I got a brand new bike for Christmas, a Raleigh Grifter, it was red, I'd never had the joy of a Chopper.

"What's a Grifter?" I asked my dad.

"A bloke who cons you out of money! Like the makers of this bike!"

Cynicism was everywhere.

Hope, that was less forthcoming, still, we'd hope for lots of snow. Trimley nestled on a hill and when it snowed those old school buses really struggled with the bank. We'd congregate towards the top and watch them with their back wheels spinning, more than 20 minutes late and that was it, we'd scoot off home.

The acne thing had done me in, I should have had a lot of friends but I felt so repulsively ugly that I could barely look at people. School photos, every year, my mugshots always looked so shameful, Mam collated all that stuff, but years later they'd cut so deep that I would tear them out from the albums and rip them into tiny pieces.

Then I started having visions, disturbing, violent, cartoon-like, they'd hit me when someone annoyed me, a snotty kid, perhaps a teacher. All of a sudden, there they were, their carcass neatly cleaved in two, swift and smooth from head to toe, a pile of flesh on the dirty floor. Woah, I thought, what's all this? I didn't ask for it to happen, I didn't want it, didn't need it, nevertheless, there it was, I prayed it was my raging hormones. I was not a violent kid, I thought I didn't have it in me, yet somehow it seemed I did, buried somewhere deep below. It wasn't any fantasy, there wasn't anyone wielding a weapon, it seemed bizarre, an abstract movie, one minute everything was fine then suddenly an abattoir. A teacher was boring me one day, next he crashed out through a window, nobody looked and nobody cared, meanwhile he just kept on talking. I felt sick, it was shocking, what if this was suddenly real, it wasn't as if I could tell anybody, what was I supposed to say? "Hey, do you get crazy visions?" You could imagine what came next. They'd have locked me up in a cell. Eric Peagerm, what a psycho! Or perhaps it *was* quite normal, hey, who could ever tell? No-one ever discussed these things, I mean, it was hardly surprising. Maybe it was the devil himself, hidden away in all of us, the good ones able to resist, the bad ones not, they'd succumb and become the murderers, the rapists.

Growing up had implications, we would watch the older boys, their ways, their actions, how they did things, we'd look up to them for cues. Our dads were from a past generation, they were distant from our world, the older boys were steeped in it, we thought we might relate to them. Sadly, they were pretty mean, they'd try to make us fight one another; purely for their entertainment, none of us were very keen but we'd oblige from time to time, we didn't want them to think we were soft. But we were smaller and thus quite weak, a gang of them captured me one day, forcing something into my mouth.

"Get a load of these, young lad!"

It was grass, or something like it, plant matter, not sure what, I choked and gagged, it tasted vile, I spat it out all over the pavement.

Another time we'd been out nesting, me and my good mate Petey Smith, a couple of older lads ran into us.

"Whatcha doin' out here?" they asked.

"Just been nesting."

"Whaddya got?"

"Nowt."

"Nowt? That's unfortunate."

"Whaddya mean?"

"I mean, y'know, y' hafta give us something or other."

One of them was evil incarnate, eyes as black as the darkest soul, the other seemed vacant, otherworldly, we were in a heap of trouble.

"We haven't got owt, honestly!"

The evil one just glared at me. He pulled his fist back, ominously, then laughed out loud and walked away.

Not so lucky next time round, there were three of us out there nesting, me, Nev Hart and Gary Jonesworth, searching through the reeds near the beck. A gang of lads appeared on bikes, I recognised one, Malcy Smarton, this was a gang of Kelton lads, though Smarty did seem fairly harmless, the rest of them looked older and wilder, the leader had a fearsome face, with scars, moustache, a prominent forehead, fairy slender but very muscular. Two brown ales on the front of his bike, in special holders, one half empty. Great, I thought. Just what we needed. Good job my companions were older, at least they could look after me.

It wasn't so.

"Run!" said Gary.

Next I knew he'd vaulted a fence, with Nev already yards ahead of him. *Shit*, I thought. Not again!

I made an attempt to climb the fence but my trousers snagged on a bit of barbed wire and before I could manage to free myself I felt a hand on top of my shoulder.

The blows came pretty hard and fast, thankfully, it didn't last long, but I was left there, bruised and bleeding, swollen face, busted lip.

Smarty, it seemed, had not partaken, he was back on the side of the road.

"I know you, Smarty!" I yelled at him.

As if *that* made any difference.

Next, something a little stranger, I'd been out in Howarth Woods, on my own, it felt much safer, I could act with independence. There was a hollow in a tree, the hole was just about face height; I peered in then I noticed something, a plastic bag, I dragged it out.

Some clothing and a note of sorts. Purple panties! Oh my goodness! Skimpy, satin, smooth and clean, I couldn't wait to read the note.

Thomas, if you beat me to it, put these on, I know you'll like them. Thinking of you wearing them excites me more than you'll ever know!

Wow, I thought, kinky bastards! Extra-marital bliss, no doubt. There were often cars parked up but I never realised what they were up to.

I read on.

You know I love you. This is more than simple lust. I crave the times that we're together.

Yours forever,
  darling,
    Trevor.

Aw, I thought. Very nice. I put the package back in the hole. Shame they had to meet this way but I guessed their lives were complicated. It was such a curious thing, what other needs did people have? I thought about it, briefly, then decided it was better not to.

Then, something stopped me nesting, I was out behind Lark View, I'd seen a structure in the bushes, had to be a nest, I thought. Couldn't really figure it out, it didn't look like any other, similar to a squirrel's drey, but lacking leaves, it clearly wasn't. I fought my way inside the bush and got my face upsides the structure, it was like a scruffy dome, made from lengthy bits of grass with a little entrance on either side. Yes, it was a nest alright, it was lined with lots of feathers, white ones, grey ones, black and brown, it looked luxurious in there. Five small eggs, sparsely mottled, quite an eerie glow about them, light from the early evening sun, glancing off mysteriously. Then, at once, a bird appeared, standing at the other side, staring at me, then the eggs, then back at me, it felt entrancing. I was amazed, a house sparrow, they would normally nest in rooves; what was it doing out in the bushes? Lack of nesting sites, perhaps? It did make sense. Sparrows were common, they would flock around the gardens, nests crowded under the eaves, the need to breed so overwhelming. That was when it suddenly hit me, this was a family, a *home*. What the hell was I doing in there? It felt as though I was intruding. More than that, I was after an egg, in other words a potential chick, I had no right to be doing this, the whole thing suddenly seemed immoral. I thought about it as I stood there, questioning what Dad had taught me, presented as a moral code, but in effect what it really meant was anything was permissible if you could somehow justify it. He was my dad, a decent man, so I would try to follow his lead, but now I was starting to question things, developing a mind of my own.

And that was it, no more nesting, I kept my eggs for a couple of years but finally I threw them out, the wildlife was much more important. It was a common theme in my life, collecting stuff then letting it go, stamps, coins, models, eggs, the urge was pretty overwhelming. I'd collect obsessively, as if I was reaching out for something, but also putting things in order, categorising, structuring. Then all of a sudden it seemed so futile, the variety was never ending, I'd decide to ditch the stuff as looking at it bored me to tears and worse than that, when I thought about it, none of it had any meaning. All at once I'd feel so empty, there was little rhyme or reason, whatever need I was trying to satisfy, in the end, it counted for nothing.

21

The family thing was quite conflicting, the ideal was so straightforward, a loving, caring collection of people, bound together by simple genetics. The reality was different, though it could be very stable, sometimes something bad would happen, blowing everything apart.

Like the death of Uncle Robbie. That one came right out of the blue, one minute he was there in his chair, the next they found him flat on his face, halfway up the hill to the club. It wasn't his death that so disturbed me, people died, I knew about that. It was something else in the aftermath, something I would never forget.

The next day it was Nanna's birthday. Cruel, I thought but what can you do? She'd lost her brother the day before. I guessed we'd have to cancel it. Wrong. Mother gave me a card. "Take this down to Nanna," she said.

"What? *Today?*"

"It's her birthday!"

"Yeah, but Uncle Robbie just died!"

"Well, this might cheer her up!"

"Doubt it!" I said. "*You* can take it."

"No, I'm really busy here, I've got too many things to do!"

And that was it, she sent me packing. Off I went with a feeling of dread. Jesus, I thought, this was stupid. Nothing good could happen here.

And I was right. First of all, Nanna's house was full of people, aunts and uncles, friends and neighbours, everybody looking miserable. Right, I thought, get it over. Say what I'd been told to say. The mantelpiece was full of cards. Maybe I was overthinking?

"Happy birthday, Nanna," I said.

I'll not forget that look on her face. A cauldron of hate and disbelief. Then she gave a bone-chilling scream.

"HOW CAN I HAVE A HAPPY BIRTHDAY?!? DON'T YOU KNOW MY BROTHER JUST DIED?!?"

She snatched the card from my hand and slung it, at least three people had to duck.

The whole room stopped and stared at me. I had never felt so bad, at least, not since Uncle Tom and *he* was there, that evil bastard.

Then, problems with our Martin, he was only four years old but that meant he was everywhere, at all times, it was so frustrating. Sharing a bedroom at any age was not without its share of problems, at thirteen the foremost problem was a serious lack of privacy! I could never mention this, who the hell would understand? Why would anyone even want to? I'd just have to suffer it. My irritation was slowly building, manifesting in various ways, whenever I held my brother's hand it felt as though I was squeezing it.

Then suddenly I discovered alcohol, I was watching the telly one night, my mother and father out at the club, my sister upstairs with a friend in her room, my brother fast asleep in ours. I heard the sideboard cabinet open, I could see an arm in there, I leapt up to investigate to find our Judy looking shocked, a bottle of brandy in her hand.

"Whatcha doing?" I enquired.

"Shhh!" she said.

"Why, who's listening?"

"Nobody! I mean, don't tell!"

Why would I? I wasn't a grass.

That was it, I was in, the moment she'd gone back upstairs, the thought had never crossed my mind but if my sister liked the stuff then maybe alcohol had some value? And it did. Not at first, it tasted pretty vile on its own, but mix it with some lemonade and the taste was almost amiable. But it was how it made you feel, relaxed and cheerful, this was the stuff. Not so available to kids, but when it was I was up for it, without the need for second guessing.

Big sis captured me one night.

"Hey ya bugger!"

"What?"

"*You* know! The drink!"

"So what? What about *you*?"

Nothing she could say about that.

We ended up filling the bottles with water.

"This is weak!" my mother would claim.

She'd look at us, full of suspicion.

"Nothing to do with *us!*" we'd say.

We stopped the watering, not the drinking.

"There was more in here than that!"

Evaporation, we insisted. Should've seen the look on her face.

Then our Judy found a boyfriend, they would babysit Saturday nights, tucking our Martin up in bed before dragging my chair in front of the telly and plonking a bottle of beer in my hand.

"Don't turn round!" our Judy insisted.

They were sat behind on the couch.

Whatever, I thought, taking a swig.

Telly and beer was all I needed.

22

I was laid on the floor one evening, gazing up at Top Of The Pops. The glam rock era was almost over, some of those bands looked pretty jaded. A song came on that caught my attention. 'Gary Gilmore's Eyes' by The Adverts. Wow, I thought, this is good! Looking through the eyes of a murderer!

"Rubbish!" said my dad from the couch.

Great, I thought, it had some value. Never knew it at the time, but this is how I discovered punk rock.

It was boring back at school, they dragged us out to a road one day, the Queen was apparently driving past and they wanted us to pay our respects. We sat there on the grassy verge. "What's the fucking point of this?" Whoever spoke got a clip round the earhole, courtesy of the cop, Scotch Jack. We hated cops. It was instinct. They were always mean to us. The following year, a lad called Jenson got a punch in the face from one for sporting an Angelic Upstarts t-shirt.

Then we had decisions to make. What to study for our exams. It was good we had a choice but choosing wasn't very easy. Teachers weren't much help, they were full of questions rather than answers; the careers bloke had a few but they were geared towards the future and few of us could envision that. At heart I was a science kid and thus I plumped for two new subjects, Geology, the study of rocks and Computer Studies, the future, right? I was forced to drop one subject, this was one of my biggest mistakes, I really seemed to excel in Biology, but as far as careers go, I was told by people who should have known better that Physics was more of a useful subject. Why the hell did I believe them? Physics was a struggle for me, but in the end I dropped Biology, maybe due to those damn dissections, something else that bothered me.

And so, boldly into the fourth year, all our classes were divided; some did O-levels, some CSEs, depending on our past performance. I was placed in 4RO, the head of form was Mr Rollinson, yes, it was an O-level class, but giving it the name of a teacher was simply playing the whole thing down. Breaks were spent the same as always, hanging around with the same old goons, my newer classmates seemed alright but maybe a little on the safe side. I got strapped along with my mates, often for things I hadn't done, but any gang would share the blame, regardless of who'd done the thing. Like stealing duck eggs from the park, by now I was beyond such things, but Terry and Venno surely weren't and five of us were caught down there so five of us were given the strap.

I was studying nine subjects, three of which were compulsory: English Language, English Lit and Maths, all of which were easy. English Lit was a bit frustrating, most of the books were pretty stuffy, Charles Dickens, he could write but why did he take so long about it? *Pages* where a line would do, the mail coach in A Tale of Two Cities, alright, it was going fast, but why the hell go on about it? Shakespeare, such exquisite plays, but no-one *ever* talked like that! Poetic, call it what you want, but mostly it was just a yawnfest. Science, that was more my bag, I always loved my Chemistry, the details took a different slant but I took the whole thing in my stride. Not so Physics. What had I done? Why the hell had I dropped Biology? I respected magnetic fields, but laws of motion, thermodynamics, conservation of energy. *What?* Mr. Stantley hated me. He was such a dry old stick. "Put that paper down, young man, and take that donkey jacket off, you won't feel the benefit once outside!" Geology was much more lively, Mr Mooney ran the show, the first thing he demanded in class was everyone put their hands up if they were only there to enjoy the field trips. Woodwork, that was reasonable, I liked it but I wasn't that good; Computer Studies, decent enough, for the most part it was easy to follow. Finally, a proper con. French. Let me tell you this. A second language is only of use if you progress to some kind of fluency. O-level French has never helped me, try and speak it over there, you'll soon be inundated with words, delivered so fast and with such ferocity that you'll *never* understand. Other cultures do have value but learning about them in school doesn't help, get out and travel, experience them, don't be wasting time with the basics. Yet again, another poor choice, I much preferred the structure of German, it was easy to understand but the German classes the year before had always been completely wrecked by one or two of my Trimley mates being utterly stupid with the teachers. Mr Horner's class especially, they would always hide his pen, they'd all take turns at getting the strap, and then, when he *tried* to get serious, they were having none of it.

"Komm her!"

Cue the combing of hair.

Another good one: "Guten Morgen."

"I'm not Morgan!" someone replied. "Morgan's sitting over there!"

Mrs Hampton got the same, she could speak both French *and* German, Scottish too, a forceful accent, nevertheless, the sad fact was that she had zero sense of humour.

It was raining hard one lunchtime, that meant we could stay in school, and since we'd all just suffered French, a few of us, five boys, two girls, decided not to bother with lunch and stay behind in the warmth of the classroom. Which got pretty boring, fast, so Finchy drew a few cartoons and the one that really tickled us was the age-old classic, the cock and balls with stumpy bristles and throbbing helmet. Neither of the girls were impressed but Hallsy had a great idea and found a little pot of glue that Mrs Hampton, for some strange reason, had stashed away in her unlocked desk. Suddenly it was stuck to the blackboard, one of those revolving affairs and wound right round till out of sight, just before a damp Mrs Hampton reappeared to kick us out.

The aftermath was very sombre, the Headmaster came around, picking us out amongst our classmates, a very shocked and upset Mrs Hampton fingering all who'd been in the room.

Then of course the interrogations, who did what, why and when. Most of us remained tight-lipped but those two girls were quite disgusted.

Finchy and Hallsy were suspended, in the end they weren't expelled, but Mrs Hampton had pushed for it so I guess the pair of them were lucky. It became a bit of a legend, Mrs Hampton's cock and balls, the only thing we did regret was not being there, in the classroom, as she wound the board around.

23

Politics. What a crock! Everyone instinctively knew it. It was confirmed one afternoon when a local MP did us the honour of turning up for a Q & A. He stood there in his pinstripe suit, trying his best to look important, not quite sure what lesson we missed but the teachers must have thought it was worth it.

Didn't answer a single question.

"What's the point of the House of Commons?"

"The situation, as we see it..."

"No! Answer the bloody question!"

"Well, you see..."

On and on. Even the teachers were unamused. No wonder the country was falling apart as we drifted headlong under these fools towards the Winter of Discontent.

It was the Summer of '78, a school trip found us up in the Lakes. 'Many seasons in a day.' It surely didn't let us down. We ended up in a record shop, a couple of mates were buying records. Top of the Pops was enough for me, oh and Revolver, loved that show; saw it up in Scotland once, my dad was doing some work up there and Mam had a cousin who lived nearby. Anyway, records. Yes, I bought one. I was averse to souvenirs, my parents had a record player so why not spice up their collection? 'She's So Modern,' the Boomtown Rats. It was dropping out of the charts but I loved the energy of that song and it had me bopping around the living room.

That was it, I needed more; I didn't get much pocket money, still, I'd spend it all on singles, there was quite a lot to choose from. Coloured vinyl pulled me in, briefly, but I have to admit it, at 14, I succumbed to marketing, I was just a pit village lad. Blondie's 'Picture This' for example, that was quite the double whammy, yellow vinyl, cool in itself, but Debbie licking a disc on the sleeve was far too much for me to resist.

I was in need of a part-time job, I knew this kid in school, Neil Powers, his parents owned the paper shop and despite him not being one of the gang I sat with him in Geology so why not sidle up to him and see if there was a job on the go?

"Why not ask in the shop?" he said.

"I'm asking *you*. You're the man!"

He looked at me, full of suspicion.

"Right, I'll get you on the list."

His mother always took the piss, a chubby lady, nice enough, she always worked in the shop on Saturdays, that was when, if I wanted anything, I'd be sent for tights for Mam, who went through those like nobody's business.

"Hiya, Eric, pearl grey, is it?"

I would hang my head in shame.

"I heard you want a paper round, is that to keep you stocked with these?"

Eventually I laughed along, I had to show her I could take it, nobody would give you a job if you couldn't take their sense of humour.

"Alright Maisie, don't get jealous, I look better than *you* in these!"

The people in the shop just stood there, trying not to imagine things.

But it worked, before too long, there I was, out on the streets, shoving papers through the doors with my little notebook of deliveries. *Sun, Echo, Sun, Echo, Echo,* I tried my best to memorise things but the weekly comics and magazine orders conspired to make such feats impossible.

Soon, Neil was part of the gang, it shocked me that he was accepted but there he was with his silly haircut, launching into a game of foulogomai. We were invited up to his house, me and Terry, Finchy and Venno. Well, why not, we thought to ourselves. That old place was quite a big one, surely there'd be lots to do?

Hide and seek was perhaps the highlight, OK, it was pretty childish, but with such a spacious house there were umpteen little hidey holes. Neil had sisters, and a brother, all of whom were older than us and rooting through their ample bedrooms sparked our curiosity.

Then, Top Trumps, that was fun, Neil had quite a lot of those; educational, sometimes profitable, often it was 10p a game. Bob, the father, caught us once. "Oh, you're little gamblers, eh?" Next we knew it was Gin or Rummy, sat around the kitchen table.

Bob would always clean us out. "What you get for gambling, see?" We suspected he was cheating but none of us had any proof. Surely it was not just skill? Either way he took our cash; it didn't stop us, not one bit, we just made sure he wasn't invited.

24

Everybody loved traditions. Something to look forward to. Some of them were quite obtuse but no-one ever questioned them. In Spring we had the Sedgeworth Ball Game, Pancake Tuesday, followed by Easter, not to mention Valentine's Day, though having such an ugly mug it wasn't that much use to me. Mothers Day and Fathers Day, the joyous pranks of April Fools Day, May Day, it went on and on, strangely there was a summer break, then Harvest Festival, Halloween.

    We all looked forward to Halloween, not because of the spooky stuff but it was a chance to make some cash, our teenage fiscal needs demanded it. While our folks were saving for Christmas, we had other things to buy, across the pond they had Trick or Treat but we had the lucrative Jack Shine the Maggie. Carve a lantern, beg for cash, we had no time for dressing up; there wasn't anything scary about it, we were focussed on the money. Still, we had to work for it, there were no pumpkins in the shops; not back then, too exotic, all we had were solid turnips. Carving those was quite a chore, they didn't have a hollow centre and younger kids were not allowed knives, imagine hacking away at a turnip with little more than a tiny teaspoon! Off we'd go, Maggies in hand, knocking on random doors in the dark, probably one in ten would oblige, the rest of them screaming: "They've already been!"

Similar thing as we hit November, now it was Penny For The Guy. Bonfire Night was fast approaching, time to collect a few old rags and try to knock up a reasonable effigy. One year we could hardly be bothered, we just dressed up Venno instead and carted him from door to door; not sure why, he could have walked!

"Penny for the guy!" we'd say.

"That's supposed to be a guy?"

"Aye, it is!" we'd all insist before giving him a kick to prove it.

It was great fun on the night, a bonfire would be built on the rec; the Council bought a load of fireworks, everybody would attend. One time it was very windy, rockets suddenly veered off sideways, some of us tried to catch the damn things as they went whizzing overhead. Then those lovely baked potatoes, they were such a revelation, there was a fire pit near the hall and the heat and the smoke would draw us in. Such a simple little meal, soft and fluffy at the centre, then that succulent charred skin, we thought we'd try and replicate it.

We'd meet up behind the garages, someone would have brought the potatoes, someone else a bunch of forks, a third perhaps a slab of butter. We'd create our own little fire pit, made from any bricks we could find, there was lots of paper and wood, those garages were a dumping ground.

"Who's got matches?"

Vacant looks. Someone would run off and get some. Hours later, patience permitting, we'd have something almost edible.

Christmas soon became monetised too, I'd ask my relatives for cash. "No selection boxes!" I'd say, "I'm getting a bit too old for that!" My parents bought me a record player with headphones so they couldn't hear and off I went on a vinyl odyssey, which would last for many years.

25

1979 my friends, the independent scene had exploded, every band was releasing a record, whether or not they were ready to. It seemed so urgent, life was short, the punk and new wave scene was expanding, post-punk hovered upon the horizon, things were getting interesting. It was very hard to keep up, second hand shops were the obvious answer, instead of wasting a quid on a single, you could get two or three for that, as long as you didn't mind the condition. Every town had at least two shops, a market stall, it didn't matter, as soon as I'd finished my Saturday papers, that was it, forget the football, I'd be off to buy records instead.

Collecting again, though this was different, records were a source of music, you could keep them in a box but getting them out and playing them was such a gratifying experience. I preferred the DIY stuff, amateurish, but full of charm, the sleeves were often cobbled together, only adding to their appeal. The Machines E.P., a masterpiece, the sleeve and labels done with ink stamps, recorded as quickly and cheaply as possible, half an hour at eight quid an hour. Coloured vinyl had lost its charm, as illustrated by The Police, I'd snapped up one of their recent singles, blue vinyl, excellent sleeve. The song was dire. Not the flipside, but I learned a couple of things: One, that B-sides were important and Two, that coloured vinyl itself meant absolutely nothing at all. The TV Personalities got it, 'Part-Time Punks,' a magnificent song, it wasn't just about the music, their ideas were important, too.

It was all a bit too much, the kids at school were mentioning albums; I had *no* spare cash for that, my paper round money, my dinner money, hardly enough to keep up with the singles!

"Where do you get the money for *albums?*"

"Nowhere."

"Whaddya mean?"

"We nick 'em!"

"What? How?"

I was told.

Shortly after, *I* was nicked.

My mother had to come down to the station. She just stood there, shocked and upset.

"What the hell did you do *that* for!"

"I dunno, I *wanted* them!"

At least she didn't tell my father, didn't dare to, he'd have been crushed; he wasn't violent in any way, but the hairpin thing suggested to me he had a lot of pent up emotion. This faux pas was pretty serious, criminal to be exact, not rooting through your mother's purse as you're convinced she doesn't love you.

It was then I got the speech, from her, the cops, from everybody, stealing wasn't a victimless crime and every crime had repercussions. They were right, I understood, I always did when people explained things; mostly no-one gave a damn, so when I was left to my own devices things would often turn out badly. What was wrong with me, I wondered, never *thought* that I was bad but sometimes I would do bad things, it felt like I was missing something. Other kids had other problems, one was expelled for punching a teacher, then a teacher punched another for inappropriate acts with a student. *I* got punched one time on the bus, one of the idiots sat in the back decided he wanted to show who's boss and demanded a look at my music paper.

"No," I said, "I'm reading it!"

Next I knew I was seeing stars.

The manly thing to do was to fight but that instinct was also missing.

26

Back in Trimley things were changing, they were building a new estate, above our street on the grassy meadow which linked us to the old church green. We enjoyed that building site, in those days there was no security, every night we'd run amuck, diving from the upstairs rooms onto sacks of insulation below. By this time we had ditched the skateboards, that had been the summer craze, we'd all had books on roller skates but with skateboards you could stand up straight and make out you were a member of Devo. We'd seen skaters on TV, performing tricks, full of grace, our bikes were all put back in the sheds as we plunged headlong, glassy-eyed, into what was sure to be that year's thing. We'd begged our mams for all the gear; helmets, knee pads, elbow pads, we needed it as what became clear was that Trimley, notwithstanding the weather, was simply not designed for such nonsense. We would spend the bulk of our time in search of a decent bit of tarmac, wandering around, looking the part, but ultimately achieving nothing as most of the paths were paving slabs and the roads were mostly full of gravel. To hell with all of that, we thought, let's risk our lives, diving from windows, smacking each other with 4-be-2s, we found it much more entertaining.

Then I discovered the John Peel show, I'd read of him in the music mags, if I was spending money on records then why not get to hear them first? I had a little radio/tape deck and earplugs not to wake my brother, I'd lie in bed, tapping my toes to some of the greatest, mind-blowing songs that I was ever likely to hear. You never knew quite what to expect, every other band was incredible, even the ones that weren't so good, I understood why others would like them. And he was so personable, a dry wit I appreciated, John was like a cool old uncle, letting you in on a special secret.

One night I was almost dumbstruck, first an ominous pounding of drums, then a bass, a slashing guitar and a voice that almost pierced right through you. Wow, I thought, what a song, an American band, the Dead Kennedys. Where would I find a record like this? Seconds later, John was telling me. Thus I bought a Postal Order and sent it off the following day, the record came within a week and I played the damn thing over and over. Even the cool kids came to hear it, they were just as amazed as me and now that mail order was a thing, the world was opening up before me.

American bands, who else was there? I asked Frank Blank at HMV, he pointed out a few on the wall.

"What they like?"

"A load of shit!"

He was wrong, so very wrong, those records were incredible, most were on the Dangerhouse label, what the hell was the matter with him? Apparently he hated Americans; the Ramones, *one* good album. Well, whatever, I brushed it off, the only problem *I* could see was I'd overlooked *his* band's new single.

"Come and see us *live*, he said."
"What? Where? At a club?"
"Yeah!"
"But I'm just 15!"
"So? You're tall. You'll get in."

The thought of it excited me, but I had never been to a gig, the cool kids had, I'm not sure how, but I had never been invited. Then I discovered a band from school, they were playing a local youthy, Dad came forward with a lift and at last I got to hear live music.

Relapse, they were pretty good; one day they would support The Jam, on top of which, quite out of the blue, I was told by one of the crowd that there was a girl who fancied me.

"Which one?" I asked.

He pointed her out.

I'd heard about her, she was a floozy. I declined, I'm not sure why, the promise of sex was quite enticing but having had nothing to do with girls I had no idea of how to get there.

What the hell had changed? I thought. Girls had never fancied me, the acne thing was still a problem and everybody said I was ugly. Maybe it was all that spot cream, it had bleached the sides of my hair, or maybe it was my shiny trousers, sexy, skin-tight PVC.

Something similar happened at school, I'd turned up in a furry jumper, yes, we had a uniform, but I was a punk, a bit of a rebel, it was good to push those boundaries.

Anyway, Deb McKaye took a shine and started running her fingers through it.

"Ooh, Eric, *that* feels good!"

"Unhand me, you lascivious tart!"

She just laughed and pulled away, I didn't know what the hell I was doing. Before I could take things any further she disappeared from the face of the earth, from school at least, apparently pregnant.

27

Then another trip to Blackpool, purely for the illuminations. They had no appeal for me, but I'd been told, on good authority, that the second hand shops and stalls were as good as anywhere in the country. But there was a little problem, someone hadn't secured enough rooms, the trip was organised by the club, and whoever was in charge of the bookings had made a right old mess of things. They asked me if I'd share a room, not with family, with a stranger, well, not a stranger as such, but a local chap who I barely knew with a rather unusual speech impediment.

Naturally I was mortified.
"Why me?" I asked.
Not enough beds.
"No," I said, "why me specifically?"
"Well, your brother's far too young!"
"I'll sleep on the floor!"
"Where?"
"*Your* room."

Mam said no, Dad kept out of it. Yet again they wouldn't say why. I'd have happily slept in the bath. My sister wasn't even there, she'd be getting pissed at home, or worse, who cared, it was all irrelevant, no-one should have had to do this. What if the guy was a raging sex fiend, what if he snored, or dribbled, or smelled? What if he did none of those things but the very fact I didn't know him was sure to mean I'd get no sleep.

Reluctantly I agreed to do it, bribed with a couple of beers at the bar. I was underage of course, but so what, I was solving a problem, it was cheap at half the price. The alcohol was sure to help, not enough to put me at risk, my roommate was a decent chap but to say I felt a little awkward was a bit of an understatement.

Back at school I was missing sports, we didn't have a football team, those P.E. teachers were so damn lazy they couldn't be arsed to put one together. The woodwork teacher finally helped, organising a couple of friendlies, it was nice to play again but so frustrating there wasn't a league. Then I tried my hand at basketball, I was asked because I was tall. Not as tall as the rest of those guys. I felt tiny in comparison. All those arms surrounding me, it was quite intimidating, I was useless, jacked it in, but I felt at one with smaller people.

Then the '70s were done, we roared into a brand new decade, we were asked to think of our future, all I could think of was buying records. My parents were invited to school, of course they declined, always did. Dad too busy, Mam didn't care. As long as my reports were good I could more or less get on with it.

The careers adviser sat us down, a serious bloke with thick white hair; he rarely said a thing to us, he'd mostly slap on a boring film then bugger off for the rest of the lesson.

This time we got one-on-ones.

"So, what would you *like* to do?"

"Dunno."

"Well, it seems you're bright. How about doing some A-levels next?"

And that was it. I was done, he scribbled something on my papers. Off I went, a bit subdued, it looked like I was staying there. It wasn't as if I wanted to, I simply didn't know what to do. I'd never had a purpose in life, it was hard enough enduring it.

Then I went to see a band, the Revillos, in a nearby town; a bunch of us invaded the bus, all leather jackets and bondage trousers. There was a crowd outside the door, it seemed the show was all sold out, a few had managed to blag their way in but the rest of us were left outside, angry at first then simply dejected. Everyone traipsed around the back and sat on a wall beside the river; we could hear the bands inside, bashing it out, tormenting us. Some went home, others stayed, somehow it seemed better than nothing, not by much but it was something, we could almost decipher the songs.

Then, at once, the back doors opened, somebody was desperate for air, they fell on through, dripping in sweat, we guessed it was pretty crowded inside. But that was it, we all sneaked in, what a view we had of the stage, the band were belting out their hits, and yes, it was crowded alright, the air was thick and full of steam, it was hard to breathe in there. Then the bouncers spotted us. Where the hell did *they* come from? We were stood at the side of the stage, cool and dry, not sweaty at all. Clearly annoyed, they bounded over, some tried squeezing into the crowd, but it was futile, it was packed and soon we were out on our arses again.

After that I craved more gigs, the atmosphere had been electric, having had a glimpse of it all, the whole thing seemed so energising. There was a rock club down in the Boro, had a bit of a reputation, still, a lot of punk bands played and the UK Subs were not only touring but they were doing a matinee show, an extra performance for the kids, on a Saturday afternoon no less. Great, I went along on the bus, a couple of schoolmates kept me company, my oh my what a gig *that* was, packed to the rafters, hot and sweaty, support bands blown to kingdom come.

I was back the following month, this time for an evening performance, Terry, who I'd known since birth, was a long-time fan of Adam and the Ants and so were two of the cooler kids. Peter Harris and Baz Redmond, turned out that they were not *that* cool, they simply seemed more sociable and hung around in different peer groups. Yet another excellent gig. No real problems getting in, my dad supplied the lift back home but it seemed the stuff the Ants were playing was veering off in another direction. They had always been an enigma, Adam loved erotic sex, bondage especially, Terry too, it was way beyond *my* understanding. They'd released a good LP, curious but interesting, now they had a tribal sound, accentuated by double drummers.

28

Should've been revising really, what with examinations looming, I would try to read my books but it was hard to concentrate. Instead, I'd be making mix-tapes, sending them around the country, swapping with all kinds of people, addresses gleaned from the music mags.

I was fond of writing letters, I enjoyed expressing myself, I'd always say a whole lot more than most could stand to listen to. Most were quite content with sound bites, insults, quips, the sharp one-liners, I demanded so much more but few would ever seem to oblige.

Then a commotion late one night, lots of shouting, banging, moaning, I proceeded to the landing, somebody was locked in the toilet. Turned out Dad had had a breakdown, too much pressure at work it seemed, as usual I wasn't told much but the whole furore was slightly unsettling.

The result, a trip to Tunisia, barely a week before the exams. I'd been across the channel before but I never thought I'd end up in Africa. Hated flying, obviously, humans weren't designed for the air and the slightest bit of turbulence convinced you, without any doubt, that in seconds you were going to die.

It was very hot out there, a dry heat that was pretty draining, generally, the entire trip was nothing short of uncomfortable. The food was strange, not bad but different, there was too much palm tree pollen, locals wanted to buy my sister, then some geezer took the piss as I was trying to mind my own business. We were accosted in the street, one of the dozens of trinket sellers, who suddenly yelled at the top of his voice:

"HEY! JOHN TRAVOLTAAAAAAAAA!!!"

I was shocked and quite confused. What the hell was he on about? Then I realised how I was dressed: black jeans and a capped black t-shirt. Oh. Right. I smiled at him, he shuffled back and nodded approvingly, then at once he spun around to face a queue across the road. The queue was for a cinema, and yes, you guessed it, *Grease* was playing, he stood there laughing and pointing at me.

"JOHN TRAVOLTAAAAAAA, ANZUR 'IILAYH!!!"

Then much worse, a horse and cart ride, it was rather pleasant at first, until the cart was hit by a taxi, not too hard but quite a jolt. What followed was a heated argument, loads of insults, mostly in Arabic, first, just between the drivers but very quickly, within seconds, dozens of passers-by joined in. It was escalating fast, somebody unsheathed a knife; more like a sword, it was scary, we scrambled out the back and ran.

Examinations came and went. We made it through the lazy summer. Most of it was spent in the fields, getting up to all kinds of mischief. We invented some crazy games, mostly pretty dangerous, setting light to aerosol sprays, things like that, decidedly mental. 'Scramble!' was a particular favourite, it evolved from a local tyre swing, someone managed to snap the rope and, failing to find a decent replacement, someone had the bright idea of hauling more tyres up in the tree and dropping them onto heads below. This was aided by the topography, that old tree was next to a bank and those below had to scramble up while others took deadly aim from above.

29

Passed my exams, all of them, two As, two Bs, the rest of them Cs. Solid, yet not *too* impressive, reasonable without revising. Not sure how I got through French, I stumbled awkwardly through the paper, most of it seemed rather silly, why did a washing line need a gender? It was onto A-levels next, Pure Maths, Chemistry and Geology, still not sure about a career, but so what, there were bands to see, the Dead Kennedys, from America, somehow had been booked in the Boro!

Or at least I thought they had, next I knew the gig was in Scarborough, begged my dad to drive me there but 60 miles was a bit too far. Bastards I thought. Fucking bastards! They'd just put an album out, I thought about a boycott in protest but that was *never* going to happen.

Sixth form was a revelation, everybody seemed grown up, the majority spoke the Queen's English, this lot didn't mess with the teachers. Chess games in the common room, no uniform requirements, it was so relaxed, I felt at ease, a good environment to study. Just as well. The subject matter, though familiar, seemed much harder, that's what A-level means, young man, *Advanced* level, what did you think? Not a problem in Chemistry, the intricate things I understood, the simplification of abstract concepts had often lacked an element of truth. Geology, I wasn't sure, much of it seemed pure conjecture, one day I'd dismiss it entirely but for the moment I was engaged. Maths was now a very mixed bag, before I'd rarely have to think, the whole thing came so naturally but now I was forced to pay attention. All the problems seemed exotic, some had elegant solutions, far too many equations of course, but that was Pure Maths, deal with it.

Prefect duty, that was a pain; monitoring doors at lunchtime, controlling who got in and out, trying to act responsible. The previous ones had been so arrogant, acting like they owned the place, I tried to play it more mature but all I ever got from it was a filthy card on Valentine's day. A fourth form strumpet sent me one, I thought it was a wind-up at first, but no, she stood there dewy-eyed, so glad that I could turn her down as she was another that soon fell pregnant.

Saw the Subs again in November, different line-up, same great show, I did miss Crass at the Rock Palladium, still, it was just as well, the local skinheads had made an appearance, beating everyone up in the bogs. I was hesitant after that, I did however see UK Decay, our Judy came with me for that one, everyone else was scared of the place.

Geology field trips, they were something, that year we went off to Aran, an island off the coast of Scotland, incredible rock formations, apparently. Those damn trips were always in winter, something of a teacher's joke. Oh, you want a *field trip*, do you? Very well, off we go! Next thing you were stood in a river, up to your waist in freezing water, sleeping in those spartan dorms, wishing you were somewhere warm. Cool kids sneaking off with the teachers, having a pint in the local pub. How'd they manage to wrangle that?

Nanna was right, "Shy bairns get nowt!"

30

1981 was a belter, got to see loads of bands that year, at 17 I was still under-age, but being over six feet tall there was never a problem gaining entry. I was buying American imports, not from HMV this time, but through the mail from California, Jello B. amongst other things had sent me a lengthy list of contacts. I was sending money orders to places like Zed and Systematic, some of those records were incredible, hit me from a different angle. Not that home grown bands weren't decent, Discharge on the Apocalypse tour, blew the roof off a Boro nightclub, made the supporting bands seem pedestrian. Then the Upstarts up on Tyneside, they were playing a secret gig, the cops had managed to stop them performing but me and Gaz, intrigued by all this, were off there like a shot on the bus. Punks were hanging around street corners, now and then you'd see a cop, it was like a game of cat and mouse, where the hell were they gonna play? We'd heard it might be up on a roof but that was too much like the Beatles, in the end they performed in a shop, a t-shirt shop of all places. "Don't nick stock!" the singer demanded, *we* complied but others refused. It was all so crowded in there, you could get away with anything. Girls At Our Best, different again, me and Terry were there this time; couldn't stop dancing, what a band, with an almost operatic singer. Hard to believe I danced that much, considering how much pain I was in, I'd spent the week potato picking, most of my muscles had all seized up. My height was useless out in the fields, bending over for hours on end, shovelling tatties into a sack while trying to keep an eye on things. You were given a number of furrows, separated by little twigs, but as the work was so exhausting your neighbours often messed with them.

Then an away day with the footie, my sister, Judy, was a regular, mostly with her best friend Pam, being members the supporters club.

Pam despised me, dunno why, no doubt I'd said something terrible, every time I opened my mouth she'd give me such a dirty look.

"No-one likes a smart arse, Eric!"

Smart arse, *me?* Surely not! Still, if I had an opinion, I was not afraid to voice it.

Anyway, there we were on the bus, me and Gaz and the rest of the gang, singing and chanting, necking cans, praying we didn't need the toilet. We were dropped off at a pub, our Judy kindly bought the beers. It was almost as good as a gig, the atmosphere was sheer electric.

This was Leeds. Lovely place. We marched along to Elland Road. Some of the locals caught our accents and started pelting us with peanuts.

Sis was having none of it.

"Stop it, NOW, you silly twats!"

Our Judy had a heart of gold but you wouldn't want to mess with her.

It was great inside the ground, away fans gathered in a corner, the camaraderie was excellent, especially when you were tanked up on beer.

Venno was there.

"What's all this? Thought you were a Hartlepool fan?"

"Aye, but me mate's a Mackem. Kindly drove us down in his van. But hey, where's Joe Jumbledon?"

"Who?"

"Y'know, Joe Jumbledon! Tough defender, saw him once. The whole of the crowd was singing his name . . . *JOE, JOE, JUMBLEDON!*"

"Oh, you daft sod, JOE BOLTON!"

"Ah!"

"He's just signed for the Boro."

"Why?"

"Because they *wanted* him."

It was goalless as half-time approached.

"Where's our Judy?"

"Over there!"

"Where?"

Someone pointed her out, behind the goal, on a stretcher. She was being wheeled away as a barrage of coins rained down from above. A steward bent over and picked them up. Nice to see he had priorities.

"How?"

"Crowd surge, banged her head."

"What happens next?"

"It depends. They'll assess her, obviously, then either let her go at the end or cart her off to hospital."

I was stumped. What do I do? My instinct was to go and help her. "THAT'S MY SISTER!" I yelled at a steward. The bastard wouldn't let me out.

"Just sit tight," Gaz suggested. "Maybe she'll be back on the bus?"

Of course, she wasn't.

Rats, I thought.

Dad was forced to come and collect her.

31

More gigs at the end of the year, Tenpole Tudor back in the Boro. Terry was turned away at the door. He was so much shorter than me.

"You're not 18."

"Neither is *he!*"

"Doesn't matter, at least he *looks* it."

It was hard to feel sorry for him. After all, he'd dobbed me in.

There was no-one in the place, the door staff had been way too strict, but luckily the band were pros and gave an incredible performance. Everyone was up there dancing, the audience, a couple of bouncers, at one point someone needed a drink, but no, he would have to wait as even the bar staff felt like dancing.

No such problems the following week, everyone was there for the Damned, they didn't turn *anyone* away, the law of economics prevailed. After a couple of terrible bands the Anti-Nowhere League appeared, no-one seemed that sure how to take to them, were they simply a bunch of bikers or just some stupid comedy band? Anyway, they incited the crowd and it was chaos during the Damned, an excellent show, all things considered, Jenson somehow falling asleep with his shaven head inside the speakers.

They were playing again in December, *Christmas On Earth*, what did *that* mean? A festival of pure punk rock in an old bus station back in Leeds. Gaz had promised to take us down, he'd somehow passed his driving test, he didn't have a car as such but his dad said, many weeks before, that should he pass he could borrow his.

Come the morning it was snowing. Dad was having second thoughts. Still, we were there on time, a young lad by the name of Adam, plus the regulars, me and Terry. We were stood there ready to go, everyone had paper rounds, you had to be careful in the snow but we weren't about to be foiled by the weather.

Still, it was pretty bad. The motorway traffic was down to 20. All that snow, massive flakes, visibility almost zero.

"Shit!" said Gaz. "Screw all this, the back roads surely have to be faster!"

They were not. Not in the slightest. We ran into a wall of snow.

The car got stuck and wouldn't reverse.

"There's some ashes in the back!"

Gaz leapt out and grabbed the bag, which ripped apart, spilling all over.

We just stood there pissing ourselves.

"Stop it!" he said. "Help me with these!"

Thus we did. Somehow or other we finally made it to the gig.

The place itself was like a bomb site, falling apart and freezing cold. Puddles of water everywhere, the bogs awash with rivers of piss.

We saw the Insane, maybe Charge and possibly one of the European bands. Then Gaz appeared, ashen-faced.

"Come on, lads, we hafta go home."

"What? Why?" We couldn't believe it.
"Didn't you hear the tannoy message?"
"No! What the hell d'ya mean?"
"Me dad's been on the phone to the venue."
"So?"
"The weather's getting worse."
"Worse? Couldn't *get* much worse!"
"I know, but it's *his* damn car!"
And that was it, the gig was over.

32

New Year's Eve in Trimley, it was soon to become my favourite thing; in previous years I'd be sat at home, watching the telly with three or four cans. The folks would roll in from the club, usually with company, it was nice to see them having fun but they were all so drunk and loud that I'd just slither off to bed. This year it was different, a mate suggested we go out, we all met up in a pub's back room, then after seeing the new year in, we wandered off on a tour of houses, having a drink in every last one. Mates houses, friends of mates, relatives, cousins, aunties and uncles, every one with a rousing welcome, those long nights seemed never ending. There was rarely any trouble, breakages occasionally, but however bad the year had been there was always hope on New Year's Eve that the following year would somehow solve it.

I was 18 shortly after, me and Terry had a party, he was born the day before me and his mam suggested we had a joint one. He lived down in Winston Square, visits there were quite eventful, whatever happened, as you left, Terry and his younger brother would wave you off with a devious grin and then dash into the kitchen and back before launching a barrage of eggs at you. We would meet there, me and Venno, Finchy and Tomo, Peter Vardy; playing records, then some cards; mostly for a bit of cash but sometimes for a bunch of singles.

"I'll raise you with a Hurry Up Harry."

"Call you with Ça Plane Pour Moi."

One time there was a hefty pot with at least six copies of Jilted John.

Anyway, a crazy party, everyone got totally smashed, not sure where the booze came from, I guessed that most had brought their own. I had never talked so much, or shouted, there was so much noise, the music was incredibly loud, the neighbours ended up calling the cops.

They turned up just as Terry's mother, Minnie, stumbled back from the club.

"Come on, you little buggers!" she said. "Party's over, everyone OUT!"

A few of us tried to hide in the bedrooms, we were just a bunch of kids; cheeky, mischievous, full of it, we'd have a drink with Minnie later.

I was ill the following day, couldn't remember much of the party; it was fun, I knew that much, but details which were always important were stubbornly eluding me. I lay there ruminating in bed, no idea how I got there, couldn't face a Sunday dinner and thus I simply had a wash and made my way back round to Terry's.

"Didn't think you'd dare!" said Minnie. She was in a dressing gown, a plump little thing, short blonde hair with tiny eyes behind thick-lensed glasses.

"Whaddya mean?"

"You don't remember?"

"Naw."

"Well, I'm not surprised."

"Come on, tell me, what did I do?"

"You really wanna know?"

"I do!"

"Well, me and Jackie Leek, and Wendy Smith, you know her?"

"Aye."

"We came upstairs to clear the rooms and found you fast asleep in the corner, slumped behind the telly table."

"So?"

"So, I said 'get up'!"

"Did I?"

"Aye, you certainly did! Then you said you needed the bog, but as we tried to guide you there you suddenly got yer pecker out and had a piss all over the carpet!"

What?!? I was mortified. Why the hell had I gone and done that? Pissed of course, but even so, I guessed that I was half asleep.

"Sorry Minnie!"

"Sorry? SORRY? Well you'd *better* be, dirty get!"

She growled but then conceded a smile.

"It was pretty funny though!"

Still, I found it hard to laugh. It was pretty shameful, really, she'd have had to scrub the carpet, *and*, even worse than that, I'd shown my cock to two of the girls! Jeez, how would I live *that* down? I was shy enough as it was, admittedly, the drink did help, but still, I wasn't huge down there and the rest of the world was soon to know it.

33

Sex was still a mystery, but now that I had turned 18 the local bars and pubs were legal, I could drink in there officially. And I did, now and then, occasionally I'd meet a girl and though I didn't know what to say I did get one or two snogs in the car park. The idea of anything more, like shagging and such, seemed pretty daunting, what exactly did you do? How did you get from A to B? Did you just undress and get on with it, or was there a special way? What you saw on the TV screen seemed either just a little far fetched or hopelessly romanticised.

I'd seen a couple of porno films, at first we'd watched some video nasties, Driller Killer, Evil Dead, I Spit On Your Gravy, that sort of thing. Then somebody would slap on the porn, the stories were hilarious, did everyone have sex like that? I wasn't sure I wanted to do it! Then a *porno* video nasty, that one made my stomach churn, involving eels, a rough-looking girl, a frying pan and a load of shit! That was verging on the subhuman, how could anyone *do* such things? I'd grown up with an older sister, I sat there feeling ashamed of myself.

Still, the world was sometimes sickening, even at a football match; mostly it was harmless fun, but one insanely cold day in winter, slagging opposing fans and the ref was trumped, in the most horrendous way, by the worst example of human scum that I'd ever encountered on the terraces. Often I would go with Gaz, chanting in the Fulwell End, but this time I was there with Dad, having shared a tasty pre-match pint to insulate against the weather. We were playing Swansea City, stood around the halfway line, watching in complete frustration as Leighton James, a Welsh international, terrorised our poor defenders, jinking his way along the flanks. It was all too much for someone, an angry, drunken, ginger chap, with wavy hair, scruffy beard and a voice that I won't ever forget.

"FUCK RIGHT OFF, YOU WELSH BASTARD!!! HOPE YOU HAVE ANOTHER ABERFAN!!!"

Hadn't a clue what Aberfan meant but it seemed that plenty other folks did.

"YOU SICK TWAT!" my father said, I'd never heard him swear like that but before I could make any sense of it, the ginger bloke, still dribbling with rage, was suddenly grabbed by the scruff of the neck and dragged off into the bowels of the stand.

It sounded like he was being murdered. I asked Dad about it later.

"What exactly was Aberfan, Dad?"

He told me, it was unbelievable.

I could hardly sleep that night. What the hell was wrong with people? There was an evil in this world that came and shook me to the core. I'd felt it in those horrible visions, dismissing it as raging hormones, but what if this was something real, something hidden in *all* of us?

34

School by now was quite a chore, Chemistry had some appeal but Geology was rather lacking and as for Maths, once so easy, now it suddenly seemed beyond me.

I would sit there with my hand up.

"Come on, Eric, *you* know this!"

I didn't. No, I fucking didn't. By the looks of it, *no-one* did.

I didn't fancy University, didn't think I'd make it at this rate, didn't like those student types; I was just a simple lad, academia wouldn't suit me. We would meet at the top of the village, shooting shit around the seats, some of the lads were already working, some had girlfriends, others bikes.

Venno had a motorbike, we'd mess around with it on Sundays, a 50cc Honda affair, we'd tank it down the country lanes. Not for long. Venno crashed it, almost hitting a car head on, instead he smashed it into a tree but somehow lived to tell the tale.

Friday night was Forbes's disco, teenage drinking at its best, as long as no-one caused any incidents, you could sit there with a beer and nobody cared, whatever your age. Snakebite rifled through our brains as the DJ played our favourite songs, punk, new wave, pop and rock, we'd all take turns to hit the dancefloor, leaping about like maniacs. I got a round of applause one night, freaking out to a Punilux song, they told me it looked choreographed but I was merely expressing myself. We all did crazy things like that. "Do The Standing Still" for instance. We'd just stand there, motionless, we didn't care if anyone got it. A local nymph was always there, she was not a pretty sight, but then so what? Neither was I, yet still, despite a few attempts she never managed to conquer me. I thought that sex was overrated, I had no experience, but animals did it, insects, mice, it was more an instinct than a necessity. Not for Ashlene, she was a tart, she lay there on a bench one night. "Jesus, somebody twiddle me nipples!"

Couldn't believe what I was seeing.

Gigs were still a welcome outlet, me and Gaz attended a few, Toy Dolls and Red Alert in the Boro, being a pair of Sunderland bands we thought it might be a little edgy. And it was, not for us, but Red Alert got their van smashed up, the Dolls meanwhile, our favourite band, could charm the pants off anyone.

Familiar with the club by now, some of us would raid the yard and grab a bunch of empty bottles, taking them back to reclaim the deposit. We'd observe the licensing laws, the bars were shut between 3 and 6, but often the main doors would be open, the bars would have the shutters down so clearly someone considered it safe. A few of us would saunter in, some would play on the fruit machine, others would wander around each room, potting balls on the snooker table or polishing off a few old drinks. Occasionally you'd find a drunk, sat asleep in a quiet corner, we would simply leave them there, it was more of a hassle to wake them up.

Then, time for more exams. Finally I began revising, *had* to, these exams were hard, so very hard that the act of revising didn't seem to help at all.

Organic Chemistry, sailed through that; nailed the practical, goes without saying. Inorganic, good enough; but Physical Chemistry, such as it was, completely stumped me on the day. I sat there staring at the paper, no, nothing, it made no sense. *Come on, Eric, write something!* Impossible, my mind went blank!

I just sat there in a stew, then all of a sudden I needed the bog, quite urgently and violently. What the hell was I going to do? A teacher was invigilating, "*On no account can you leave the room!*" Those were his exact same words. To hell with it. I escaped.

There was quite a kerfuffle next day.

"You handed in a blank sheet of paper!"

"Yes, I did!"

"Why, though, *why?*"

"I needed the bog,"

"Put your hand up!"

"But we were told . . ."

"Never mind that! Toilet breaks can be arranged! You simply have to be supervised!"

Then why the hell not *mention* it?!?

I felt let down. Worse, betrayed. There was no way I could resit, not unless I waited a year and who had any time for that? Chemistry was my strongest subject, now I'd surely fail the exam. They didn't take an average score, you had to succeed in all four sections.

All the other exams were crap, my heart just simply wasn't in it. Geology was passable, but Maths, oh that fucking Maths, like wading through a bloody swamp!

One of the teachers grabbed me beforehand.

"Raise your hand if you need a shit!"

I didn't because I just didn't care. I wanted out, immediately.

35

Things were pretty flat after that. What the hell was I going to do? I had an interview lined up but after those disastrous exams there wasn't a chance that they'd employ me. Then my dad thought he could help, he knew a local businessman who'd played some football back in the day and looked a bit like Terry Thomas.

So, he drove me down to his office, somewhere in the heart of Monkton, I just sat there mystified as Gentleman George, as he was known, assaulted me with a barrage of questions. They had nothing to do with work, I should have asked him what he did but since my father hadn't told me I'd assumed it wasn't relevant. But it was, *of course* it was; that's why I was sitting there, I didn't know *what* to ask or say and Dad just hadn't thought to tell me. What did people think I was? Clever? Savvy? Bloody psychic? I knew *nothing* about the world. I was desperate for guidance.

I consoled myself with records, they were all I could relate to, there was wisdom in those songs though little that would help me find a bit of purpose in my life. Most of it was tear it down, the world's a mess, let's all go crazy; honest, heartfelt, passionate, yes, but what would we replace it with? No idea. It was useless. Give the kids a chance. Oh really? Give the kids a chance to do what, the same things that their parents did? At least I had an interview, maybe *that* would teach me something, it was on the south coast somewhere, maybe it would open my eyes? Or maybe I could just say screw it and leave the bloody train in London, wandering off into the crowd to assume a life of unbridled debauchery? Who could tell what lay ahead? I was young and full of energy, all I needed was a focus, surely *that* was not beyond me?

Other titles in the Trimley Trilogy:

SCHEMES - a novella - the missing link

Eric struggles to find that focus. Five long years of desperation. Sex, drugs and rock 'n' roll, with some abandon, pit village style.

DELIVERY - a novel - the first installment

Continues right where *Schemes* left off, the flat, desolate, full of frustration. Then, at once, a second chance. Will Eric make the most of it?

Kindle versions available on Amazon

Paperbacks, while stocks last, from:

peagermpress@gmail.com